STAR PROTECTORS

MY ALIEN MATES BOOK 3

MAGGIE ALABASTER

"CAPTAIN, there's a ship approaching. It's the *Chimera*."

"What?" I shot up straighter. "Are you sure?"

For three weeks, Brinley and I had been at Undapan Station, waiting to hear those words. Now, my heart was in my throat. My stomach twisted into knots.

Brinley laughingly referred to the station as Underpants, but I hadn't felt much like laughing since *Chimera* disappeared in the window, taking Slek and Zarex with us. J'avet forbade me from going with them to help rescue Danec. For that, I wanted to hate the commander. Honestly, I was almost as worried about him as I was about the others.

Almost.

Equally, I wanted to knee him in the groin. From what Slek told me about J'avet's pubic plate, it would hurt me more than him.

I shook my head to clear it and focused on the station's lieutenant.

Technically, I wasn't supposed to be in the station's command centre, but they hadn't stopped me from entering the day Brinley and I arrived. As long as I helped in the infirmary when I was needed, no one cared what I did with my spare time.

Honestly, I had a feeling Zarex sent word ahead to let me in if I asked. That seemed like the kind of thing he would do. The guy knew what I needed better than I did.

"I'm sure." The lieutenant barely gave me a glance. "They're giving off a distress signal."

My face jerked toward her. I wanted to ask more, but I bit my lip instead. Now was time to keep my mouth shut and let her concentrate.

See, J'avet, I have learnt some restraint, I thought. I wouldn't mind if he rolled his eyes at me right now. At least he and the others would be here with me.

The station's captain, Vaw, exchanged looks with the lieutenant. An Agusian man, he could pass for a shorter, stockier version of Zarex.

"Open communications," Vaw ordered.

"Yes, sir." The lieutenant, I think her name was Karji, nodded. She tapped buttons on the screen in front of her.

"*Chimera*, this is Undapan Station. Do you require assistance?"

I held back a smile. I suppose the name was a *bit* funny. Still, it wasn't nice to make fun of other planet's languages. Apparently 'elbow' in English translated into Blarvian as 'penis.' That might be awkward in the wrong context.

My smile faded when I realised there was no response from *Chimera*.

"Life signs?" Vaw asked.

Karji tapped her screen again.

I curled my hands into fists until my nails dug into my palms. The anticipation was painful.

No doubt Slek was currently trying to fix the communications system and turn off the distress signal. He'd have a good laugh about all of this when they arrived.

"A lot of fuss for little ol' me," he would say. He was neither little nor old. Or modest for that matter. He'd probably enjoy the fuss for a while.

Zarex—he would smile.

Danec too. He must be back to himself now, after

the others purged the nanobots from his system. Right?

That fantasy was rudely blasted to smithereens when Karji replied.

"Just one, sir."

One? What the fuck?

I gaped at her.

"That can't be right," I said. "The *Chimera's* crew —" A couple of hundred people of various species should be on board. And my guys.

"—should number higher," Vaw finished for me. "Are you certain, Lieutenant?"

"That's what my screen says, sir," Karji said.

"Can you tell who?" I asked.

"No," she replied simply. "*Chimera* looks to have taken some damage."

I peered at the screen which showed her closer than the window would have. My stomach twisted tighter. The small ship showed a scorch mark down one side. Beside that was a huge dent. What the hells caused that? Road rage incident? Well, space rage. It seemed unlikely the *Chimera* hit a tree.

"Nurse, you should make your way to the docking area," Captain Vaw said gently. "Whoever is aboard might need your help."

"Sir, should they be allowed to dock?" Karji asked. "It might be a nanobot trick."

I held back an angry response.

Vaw spoke instead. "You implemented the new life sign search which can detect Iritauri?"

Slek had developed it. Apparently he'd had time to pass it on before he left to chase the nanobot hosts. Called Iritauri, or Iri, they were usually Freytaurians who were invaded by bots, their minds taken over against their wills. They turned silver and often walked around with glazed expressions and blasters.

"Yes sir," Karji said without inflection. "It detected no Iritauri, or nanobots."

"Then we will take the risk," the captain concluded. He nodded toward me. "However, if the scanner doesn't work, Nurse Wright is the best person to send, since the bots don't like human bodies."

There was no accounting for taste. In this case, it worked in my favour. The nanobots *might* now be modified so I could become a host, but the last time we met, my blood made them dormant. I could only assume that was still the case. And hope like hells.

I nodded. "On my way." I headed toward the

door, then stopped. "Can you ask Pilot Brinley Grant to meet me there, please?"

Brinley should have gone on to the study facility at Agus, but like me, she refused. She spent time in the station's pods and on the bridge of every passing ship which would let her. Right now, only a few ships were docked at the station, so I knew she could spare the time. Even if she couldn't, she would drop everything for this. The guys were her family as much as they were mine.

Vaw nodded. "I'll see to it," he said. His smile suggested he didn't mind me bossing him around, just this once.

I flashed a smile and hurried out the door.

Undapan Station was huge. At least twice the size of Moon Station. Maybe bigger than Dendra Station.

My boots clicked on the floor as I trotted toward the docking area. I kept an eye out for a transport cart, but none passed. Like a golf cart or a forklift, they carried people and supplies all over the station. It would save the walk, but hunting for one would use time I couldn't waste.

I puffed lightly as I drew to a stop outside the docking bay doors. They stood about twice my height and several times wider. Big enough to fit a lot of things through at the same time, but not enough for a pod or ship, if they were off course that badly. Of course if a ship collided with the station, the door wouldn't save us.

Hoping I hadn't just jinxed the place, I pressed my hand against the palm pad beside the door. After a moment, the pad flashed green and the doors slid open.

"Thank you," I told them as I stepped through. Just because the doors weren't alive didn't mean I shouldn't be polite. Or maybe I was a little stir crazy after the long wait for this day to arrive. Waiting for my guys.

Until I saw the *Chimera*, and looked inside, I wouldn't accept that they weren't on board. Something weird was up, for sure. Hells, something always was. I hoped it wasn't something sinister as well.

"Hey." Brinley trotted to catch up and slipped her hand into mine. "They're finally back?"

I told her what the lieutenant said. She stopped walking and frowned.

"One life sign? That's odd." Her English accent was stronger when she was worried.

"That's one word for it," I said. "Fucked up being another."

She smiled. "That too. I'm sure it's a mistake."

"I'm worried that if it is a mistake, it's because the ship is swarming with Iri," I said. "They might have figured out how to counteract Slek's Iri-finder."

Her tongue darted across her lips. I knew what she was thinking. The easiest way for them to have done that was if Slek was Iri now too. If that was the case, J'avet would be lucky if I only punched him in the head. He was the one who insisted on Slek and Zarex accompanying him on the mission.

And leaving me out.

That still rankled something fierce. If there was any chance I might have helped, he had robbed me of it. And robbed Slek of his Freytauriness.

Okay, I was being unfair. If Slek was Iri, it wouldn't be because J'avet let it happen. Someone had to go after Danec with him and Slek was an obvious choice.

One thing I knew for sure, if Slek was a host, he would be pissed off about it. He'd made his thoughts on becoming a host very clear. Although, so had Danec, and the last time I saw him, he had silver skin and glazed eyes. He was all Iri, or almost. I knew the real him was still in there somewhere, I was certain of it.

Or at least…he was a month ago. He *had* to still

be in there now. I wouldn't accept he was lost to me forever. Not until I knew for certain.

"If they are Iri, we just have to make sure they don't make it past the front door," Brinley said firmly. "Security is waiting." She nodded ahead.

Sure enough, there in the docking bay stood no less than six security officers, blasters already in their hands.

A woman, who I guessed was their leader, nodded to me and jerked her head toward a screen on the wall. On it, we could all see *Chimera's* slow but steady approach.

"It should only be a few minutes longer," she said.

"Great," I said, and forced a smile that likely looked like I needed to pee. I was too anxious and scared for a genuine smile. In a few minutes, with any luck, I would have a few smiles to spare.

I glanced around at the security officers. They were all intent on the screen. One or two bounced on their heels. It might be excess adrenaline, but not much happened on the station. This could be the first excitement they'd had in a while.

What did they do in the meantime? I wondered. Folks could only do so many laps of the place, or play so many games of chess.

A person couldn't read too many books, but I hadn't

seen any of the officers in the library, so maybe books weren't their jam. Shame, books are the best, amiright?

I startled when, three or four minutes later, the space doors clanged open.

An hour or seven passed—okay, three or four more minutes—and they closed again.

Everything froze.

Time.

My heart.

Everyone's movement.

Every sound.

Beyond the docking bay's doors, something beeped and time started up again.

My heart remained stopped— Oh no, it started again. Now it pounded as the docking bay doors slid open.

The *Chimera*, big as she was, looked small parked inside Undapan's bay. Her long legs were splayed out to the sides, all three of them.

"There should be four," Brinley remarked. She sounded as concerned as I felt.

"Shit," I muttered. Closer up, *Chimera* looked like someone shoved a stick in her and held her over an open flame. The scorch marks were more pronounced and looked much worse. Unlike an *actual* marshmallow, she hadn't melted, but someone had certainly given it a good try.

"Stay a good distance back," the security officer said. She'd clearly heard Brinley and was concerned the ship might topple.

Not wanting to be squashed like an ant today, or indeed any day, I stepped just inside the door and stopped.

I was about to ask what happened next, when *Chimera* shuddered. A ramp began to lower out of the side of her.

I swallowed and found my mouth dry. I stood on my toes and tried to look inside the ship for the guys. All I saw was darkness. A never ending hole of nothing.

"Hello?" I called out.

I waited for the guys to answer. No response came. Not even a smartass remark from Slek. No innuendo, no flirting. Just silence.

"Should we go inside?" Brinley asked.

The security officer held up her hand and waited a moment longer. Before she said a word, a sound came from inside the ship. A shuffle, followed by a groan.

"It sounds like they need help," I said. I wasn't

ready to accept it might not be *any* of the guys. That they might be—

No, they *had* to be alive. If they weren't, I would find them in whatever came after life and kick their asses.

"Something is coming out," one of the other security officers said.

"Or someone," Brinley said firmly.

A figure appeared in the doorway. He staggered down the gangway, hand pressed to a bandage on his head.

J'avet pressed something into my hand before he collapsed at my feet.

2

I ADMIT IT, my first instinct was to drop whatever he handed me, and run. Explosive devices didn't tick anymore, but neither would a handful of nanobots.

Once I'd resisted the urge, I opened my palm and glanced down. It looked like a computer chip.

I thought about handing it to the security officers, but their eyes were on J'avet and the *Chimera*.

I quickly tucked the chip into my pocket and knelt beside J'avet.

His hand fell away from the bandage, allowing me to peel it back slightly. I sucked in a wince.

The wound on his head was shallow, but long and ugly. At first glance, it didn't seem to be infected, but it would leave an epic scar.

I replaced the bandage and turned my attention

to the rest of him. He looked pretty beaten up. Fading bruises covered his face and what I saw of his neck. A long cut ran from near one eye, all the way down to his chin.

"We need to get him to the infirmary," I said. "I'll give him a full body scan to check for nanobots, then the doctor can treat his injuries."

The head security officer nodded. She waved for the others to bring a gurney which sat off to the side of the docking bay.

They wheeled it over and pressed a button on the side, which lowered the top of the gurney to the ground. From there, they carefully moved J'avet onto it, then brought it back up and walked away in a hurry.

None, I noticed, was a Freytaurian. I hoped their caution was misplaced. If the nanobots could make anyone a host, we'd all be in for a galaxy of trouble.

I placed a hand on the trackpad at the end of the gurney and guided it toward the door.

They say modern technology is supposed to make life easier, but I would have preferred an old-fashioned handle. One I could grip and push the thing around. A slip of a finger on the trackpad and the gurney would move sideways, or run into a wall.

Yep, they still haven't perfected the shopping trolley.

Brinley walked beside me, with half the security officers behind. The other half stayed with *Chimera*.

I presumed they would check her over for— I didn't want to think they might find dead bodies on board. Nope, I was not going to go there unless I was told implicitly they'd found some. Even then, I would have to see for myself.

"What do you think happened?" Brinley asked.

I looked down at J'avet and shook my head. "I don't know, but it's nothing good. Hopefully he'll be able to give us some answers soon."

It was all I could do not to shake him awake and demand them. I wouldn't give in to emotion. Doing that could kill him. He was an asshole, but I didn't want him to die. Quite the opposite, for some reason.

I needed him to live, and it was more than just wanting answers. He was the last person in the universe I should give two fucks about, but seeing him lying there…

Only the rise and fall of his chest and shallow breathing told me he was alive. If I had it my way, he would stay that way for a long time.

"The others will be fine," Brinley said. "They're

probably on a pod, a few hours behind. You know how J'avet is. Maybe he wanted to make a dramatic entrance."

I snorted softly. "If anyone was going to kick everyone off a ship to make himself look good, it would be him." Only...even he wasn't that big a jerk. I knew Brinley was trying to make me feel better, so I did my best to play along. The effort was half-hearted at best.

"Edie..." Brinley said gingerly.

"I'm okay," I said quickly. "We need to concentrate on J'avet right now." By 'we' I meant me. Professionally, my patient deserved all of my attention. Personally—that was something I didn't need to think about right now.

"Of course," she said.

I turned my face to glance at her. "I'm sorry. I know this is as important to you as it is to me. They're your family too."

"The guys are like brothers," she said. "You're like a sister. If you hurt, I hurt. If they're in trouble—"

"You'll come with me to punch some mother-fuckers?" I suggested.

She responded with a low laugh. "Yes, exactly. Or blaster them, at least. My right hook leaves something to be desired."

"I'm sure it's awesome," I told her. "But you're right, blasters are easier."

J'avet groaned and shifted.

"Stay still." I wasn't sure if he could hear me, but I got some petty pleasure from bossing him around for a change.

He stopped moving. Although it probably had nothing to do with me, I nodded in satisfaction.

"Good. Keep still." He might have broken bones or internal injuries. To have him die on the way to the infirmary would suck. "We're almost there."

It felt like days, but it was only a handful of minutes before I guided the gurney through the doorway. I didn't even hit it into the wall.

Go me.

While the doctor on duty, a nervous-looking Freytaurian, stood back and watched, I manoeuvred the gurney toward the body scanner. Someone already had the forethought to move the bed which usually lay underneath it. All I had to do was guide the gurney into place and turn the scanner on.

Finger on my lips, I watched as it slowly made its way from his feet, all the way up to his face.

"Several broken ribs. Blaster burns." Those looked painful. He must have changed his shirt at some point, they weren't visible on the one he wore now.

"Severe dehydration, empty stomach. Minor head wound. No sign of nanobots." I double checked his teeth, but none hid in there.

The entire infirmary let out a collective sigh of relief.

The doctor, a blue skinned man named Barek, stepped forward.

"Bring him over to the examination room. We'll get him on a bed and have a good look over him. We'll start with IV fluids. Nurse, get me a bag."

I nodded and went to do as I was asked, as though a moment ago I wasn't their last line of defence between them and a nanobot invasion.

I grabbed a bag out of the fridge, while the doctor selected the right antibiotics and anti-inflammatories for a Parvoran.

As far as I knew, J'avet could take the same medicines as I could, but I wasn't certain enough to make that call. I mean, if I had to, I would. Okay, I would consult the database, then decide what to give him.

Doubtless, Doctor Barek had done this a hundred times before.

I set up the bag on a pole and hovered nearby while Barek slid a needle into J'avet's arm.

"He should be fine," the doctor said. "Looks like he hasn't had sufficient fluids for at least a week."

I frowned. "*Chimera* should have water—"

"Yes, she should," he agreed.

I heard the inflection in his tone and nodded. Intimate knowledge of the ship's food and water stores weren't within his skill set. Fair enough. They weren't mine either.

"Any idea how long it might be before he wakes?" I asked.

"It depends on the head wound." Barek nodded toward it. "Remove the bandage and wash it."

"Yes, Doctor." I hurried to get a basin of water and some cloth.

"He'll be okay?" Brinley asked. She hovered near the door, looking worried.

"He's got a hard head," I said. "I'm sure he'll be yelling at us all this time tomorrow."

She smiled briefly and stood back against the wall, where she'd be out of anyone's way.

As gently as I could, I peeled back J'avet's bandage. It was covered in dried blood, and didn't smell too clean.

He twitched as I worked the last corner loose.

"Sorry," I said, even if he couldn't hear me.

I threw the bandage in the bin, then washed my

hands before I started to wipe away the blood caked around the wound.

"Ouch, that looks painful," I said. It didn't look life-threatening to me, thankfully.

"Indeed." Barek finished with the IV and two different needles, then moved to where he could see better. "We'll glue him back together."

Not actually glue, he secured a tube from a shelf and an applicator and started to apply a clear substance to J'avet's head. It would form a kind of shell that would allow the skin underneath to heal quicker.

The shell would give him an even harder head than usual. At least on that part. His head would match his pubic plate. That idea almost made me laugh and I had to bite it back.

"Get some scissors," the doctor said. "Remove his clothing." He nodded to another nurse to help.

Okay, I won't lie. More than once I imagined taking off J'avet's clothes, but not with scissors. Usually it involved fingers and maybe teeth. What? My imagination is creative, okay?

I started at the hem of his pants, while the other nurse cut into one of his sleeves.

His legs seemed more or less intact, the short red

fur lay undamaged but needing a good, long soak in a nice, hot bath.

My knuckle brushed past the front of his thigh and I marvelled at how soft he felt. I could have patted him for ages, except for the whole thing about him loathing my guts. I was big on consent.

I tugged at the fabric and it tore all the way up to his waistband. Everyone should rip fabric once in a while, it's therapeutic.

I cut his waistband and his pants fell away, revealing tight, white underwear. Big surprise, right? I mean, I wasn't expecting *Transformers* or *Spider-man*, or anything like that. A thong, maybe? Naw, he had a stick up his ass, not a piece of fabric.

Recognising this as an entirely inappropriate line of thought towards a patient, I shoved the musings away and went to get a basin of clean water. While he was mostly naked, I would sponge J'avet off. He'd likely prefer to wake up clean. I know I would. Dirty on the inside, clean on the outside. Unless you're talking about covering someone with chocolate. That was a different story.

Yeah, I hadn't gotten laid in a month and it showed. The guys had spoiled me before that, in the best possible way. Now my body ached to be touched, filled, wet.

"Oops." I slopped a little bit too much water on J'avet's leg. I cleaned it up while the doctor glanced at me. He'd finished with the glueing and was now clicking his tongue at the scorch marks on J'avet's chest.

"Singed the hair," Barek said. "And the skin. He was incredibly lucky. He should go and bet on the durva races."

I smiled.

I knew from Slek and Danec that durva birds had big teeth and loved to stop mid-race to bite each other, then bury their way into the ground and disappear. The chances of betting on one who actually finished, much less won, was incredibly difficult. So of course, it was one of the more popular pastimes on Frey-T.

"All in all, he's in reasonable shape, for someone who took a beating," the doctor concluded. "We will need to wait for him to wake up before we can determine if any lasting damage was done to his brain. Someone must be on watch at all times."

I nodded. "I'm not busy. I'll stay with him." It wasn't because I cared about him at all. No way. I just...happened to be unoccupied. Nothing more.

"Good." Barek moved toward a data station and

slipped in behind the chair. No doubt to enter J'avet's details into the database.

I cleaned up around J'avet's bed and washed my hands.

Only as I turned off the water, I remembered the chip he handed me before he'd collapsed.

3

I GLANCED over my shoulder before I pulled the chip out of my pocket. I gave it a closer look. To my untrained eye, it looked like nothing special. Slek would probably tell me the specifications down to the last decimal point, but it would be meaningless to me.

I placed the chip under a small scanner. Designed to look more closely at head wounds, broken fingers and antennas, using it hopefully wouldn't draw too much attention.

I peered at the screen and exhaled softly. As far as the scanner could tell, it was bot-free. Hopefully it wasn't infested with something worse.

"I wondered what he slipped you," Brinley said over my shoulder.

I jumped. I hadn't even seen her approach. Lucky I hadn't gone into spying as a profession. I would suck at it.

"Yeah, it's J'avet," I said. "He wouldn't slip me anything good."

She stifled a laugh with her hand. "We should probably take that to the captain."

I ran a hand over my crazy curls. The ones on my head. "I suppose we should. I just…" I glanced back toward J'avet. "He wanted me to have it for a reason. He could have given it to security."

Brinley looked apologetic before she said, "Or you were the closest person."

I lowered my hand to my lap. "That's possible too," I agreed. "I might be reading too much into this. It is J'avet after all. Given a choice, he'd give it to anyone but me." I said the words, but I didn't believe them. He had staggered toward me. He looked at *me*, albeit only a fraction of a glance. I was sure he meant it for me.

"We could put it into a computer and find out," I said. "One not connected to the rest of them."

"Right. It might have a nasty virus J'avet didn't know about." Brinley looked thoughtful. "Just a wild guess there isn't one like that here."

"I wouldn't think so," I agreed. "Slek would know."

"So would the captain," she reminded me.

"When did you become such a goody goody?" I asked teasingly.

She smiled faintly. "Since we all almost died. I'd prefer that not happen again."

The uncertainty in her eyes matched my own. This chip might contain a virus, or the answers as to whether or not the guys were alive.

"I think I can find us a tablet where the chip should fit inside," Brinley said slowly. "I'll get it and bring it back here. I'll try not to be long. Maybe hide that until I get back. If we hand that to the captain, we may never find out what's on it."

I swallowed hard and nodded. "That's true. That would suck." We'd get the whole 'don't worry your pretty little heads about it' spiel and that would be that. We'd be lucky if we ever found out what, if anything, the IF did about what information was on there. That didn't sit right with me at all.

"I need to check on the patients," I said. I pulled the chip out and tucked it back into my pocket. If J'avet would wake, it would save a lot of trouble and speculation, but he was still out.

He looked so peaceful lying there, but part of me wanted to give him a hard poke to wake up.

I resisted the temptation. He needed to rest. Time for answers would come soon. Not soon enough, but soon.

I walked around the infirmary, checking on the handful of patients who were currently resting there. Most had broken bones, or had just given birth. Most inflictions were healed so quickly these days, no one stayed for long.

By the time I'd made a coffee for one patient and changed the sheets for another, Brinley was back, tablet in hand.

We sat down near J'avet and tried to look as though we weren't up to anything suspicious. I was sure we didn't quite pull it off, but no one gave us a glance.

I pulled out the chip and pressed it into the port of the tablet. Brinley turned it on and we waited.

After a moment, the tablet screen showed a file icon for the video.

Brinley and I exchanged glances before she pressed the icon.

My heart jumped when Slek's face came onto the screen.

"If you're watching this—" He ducked out of view.

"Fuck, that was close." The vision shook and something behind him rumbled. "There's a lot of Iri here. Too many to..." The screen crackled and several words were cut off. "Putting coordinates on this chip. Get it to the IF... main headquarters..." He was breaking up badly now.

"Too many to stop at once... Need to get inside. We're gonna try..." The screen crackled again. Slek glanced over his shoulder, then back at the screen and smiled.

"Zarex says hello."

The whole screen seemed to shake, then the video ended.

"Shit," I breathed. "There should be another file on there."

Brinley closed the video and searched through the files for a moment. "There's a small file, but it won't open." She pressed on it a couple of times. "It might be password protected."

I frowned toward J'avet. "He might be the only one who knows it. Unless we can guess."

"I don't think it will be '123456,' or 'sexypants,'" Brinley said.

I barked a short laugh. "Probably not. Knowing him, it's something obscure." I sighed. "Slek would be able to hack it."

"Maybe Slek put the password on there," Brinley suggested. "Something only you would know."

I thought, but drew a blank. I had no idea what he would choose, that I would remember. He had no cutesy nickname for me. I didn't have one for him either. Danec called him Slekie once.

I took the tablet from Brinley and right clicked on the icon. An option to put in a password popped up. I keyed in 'Slekie' and pressed return.

The screen responded with, 'Incorrect password.'

I ran a hand over my hair and tried, 'Danny', Slek's nickname for Danec.

"That's wrong too," I said, frustrated. I tried a few more words, including 'orgasm' and 'sex'. I even tried 'puny,' which I used to tease him and his enormous muscles.

"I'm starting to think I don't know him," I said, frustrated.

"What about where you met?" Brinley suggested.

"On board *Infinity*." I tried that. Still nothing. I keyed in 'Kalvix,' the doctor who he flirted with, but who was later killed, a causality of the conflict between the Freytaurians and the Iritauri.

The file opened.

"Holy shit!" I said, louder than I intended. There on the screen was a series of numbers. "We did it."

"*You* did it," Brinley said. "The question is, what do we do with it?"

I closed the file and handed the tablet back to Brinley. "We go after them," I said firmly. "Slek wanted to let us know where to look." If he and Zarex had gone in themselves, they might be dead now, or worse, hosts.

"If they got the chance," Brinley said. "That video… They might have been taken before they could try anything."

"All the more reason for us to go looking," I said. After a moment, I added, "You don't have to come."

"Can you fly a ship?" she asked.

I hesitated. "I could learn," I said finally.

"*You* don't have time to learn," she said. "I'm coming. On one condition, and it's not negotiable."

I looked at her sideways. I trusted her implicitly, but I was always doubtful when anyone put conditions on things.

"What is it?" I asked carefully.

"We have to wait for J'avet to wake," she said. "He knows what happened. We need to see what he has to say before we go off half-cocked."

"I always prefer to go off full-cocked," I said absently. "Fine, that's a good idea."

I was also eager to see if he was okay or not. I

mean, not *too* eager. It was professional courtesy, that's all. Yep, that was it. I didn't care about him in any other way. Okay, maybe a little. He kept life interesting, even if he was an infuriating moth-erfucker.

I stood and gave him a once-over. The IV seemed to be doing its job; restoring fluids to his body. His breathing was deeper now, stronger. If he'd arrived a day or two later, it might be a very different story. He'd be dead and the captain would have the chip. The IF might not have the coordinates, but they'd know the mission went badly. They'd probably send in a fleet of ships with lasers and destroy everything in that part of the galaxy. Maybe they should do just that.

A sensible person would go straight to the captain and give him the chip. I could go on to Agus and forget about all of this.

The very idea was absurd. As if I was sensible, or had a selective memory. No, I would wait until J'avet woke up and go from there.

What, I asked myself, *will you do if he wants to take the chip to the captain?*

Myself, I replied, *I have no idea.*

I had to cling to the thought that J'avet wanted me to have the chip so we could act. Because, I reminded myself, he thought of me as a hothead, who couldn't contain her emotions. He said he didn't like that about me. I think maybe he lied. Or now he was trying to monopolise on my rashness. Why though?

Hells, I could speculate all day and never come to a conclusion.

"If he was me, I'd wave coffee under his nose," I said. "Or chocolate. That would wake me up."

Brinley grinned. "Me too. Or a glass of rum."

I grimaced. I was more of a wine girl myself, but each to their own.

"Maybe we should wave some beer under his nose," I said. I had no idea what he drank, or even if he drank, but the smell was pretty strong.

"Or we could wait patiently," Brinley said.

"Bah." I waved dismissively. "If we keep talking, he'll wake and tell us to shut up."

"Now that sounds like him," Brinley agreed. "He isn't much on small talk."

"He really isn't," I agreed. "Or talk of any kind. He prefers to growl and glower." I was babbling on, with one eye on J'avet. With any luck, he would hear and get annoyed.

"Yes, he's good at glowering," Brinley agreed.

"The best. I've never seen a better cranky face than his."

Brinley looked like she was enjoying herself way too much here.

I was too, to tell the truth. It was nice to tell J'avet what I thought about him, without him responding angrily. Unless he could hear, in which case, I was probably in for it any moment now.

I cocked my head at him, but he did no more than a twitch. I couldn't rule out the possibility his head wound was worse than the doctor thought.

J'avet might never regain consciousness. In that case, what would Brinley and I do? Her condition would be out the window. Honestly, as badass as we were, I wasn't sure the two of us were equipped to take on an army of Iri.

I turned to face J'avet. In my sternest voice, I said, "Listen here, you arrogant jerk. We have better things to do than sit by while you sleep. You need to get your shit together and wake the hells up. You didn't limp all the way back here, on a ship, alone, without a perfectly good reason." Gods help me, I needed to know what it was.

I used Slek's favourite words. "Stop being a gwarp and wake up."

J'avet stirred. At first it was just a small, sharp

move of his head. Then his eyelids flickered and his mouth drew back.

I stepped closer, until my nose was a handspan or two from his face.

"J'avet?" I said. "Come on, you can do this. We need you to wake up."

His nostrils flared and his eyelids flickered again.

He let out a long, slow, pained breath. Then, without opening his eyes, he said, "Would. You. Shut. Up."

I couldn't help it. I threw myself over his chest and hugged him.

4

"You should be on Agus by now," J'avet said between spoonfuls of soup. Doctor Barek wouldn't let him eat anything more substantial.

"He hasn't consumed a proper meal in too long. His stomach will reject it," Barek said firmly.

The IV would fill him up as well, so I didn't argue. To my surprise, neither did J'avet. Maybe because it was the doctor's orders and not mine.

"Aren't you lucky I'm not?" I retorted. "You'd have some other nurse bossing you around."

"And you'd be safely away from here," he said evenly.

"You're worried about my safety?" I asked. I fixed him with a level glance. If he had something to say, now was his chance.

He shovelled another couple of spoonfuls into his mouth and shrugged. "I'm concerned for the safety of everyone in the IF," he said finally.

"Right," I said. He was frustrating, but that was nothing new.

"For what it's worth," he added, "I was worried about you. You're good at getting into trouble."

"It's a skill," I said dryly. "I have a few of them."

"I'm sure you do." He actually smiled, albeit faintly.

"How does your head feel?" I asked.

"It doesn't hurt, currently." He looked as though he wanted to ask something, but stopped as another nurse walked past.

When she was gone, I said, "Brinley and I watched the video."

I licked my lips. Here came the bit I didn't want to ask, but I *had* to. I'd held it back for long enough.

"Are the others… Are they alive?"

J'avet exhaled. "I don't know. After Slek made that recording, he hid the chip under the navigation console. The Iri attacked and *Chimera* was boarded. We fought back, but there were too many of them. I was knocked out. When I came to the ship, it was empty."

He closed his eyes and looked pained. "*Chimera*

was being towed toward Tarathu. I managed to break the ship free and evade them. I knew I needed to get that chip back to the IF."

My heart ached for what they all went through, and for the expression of despair on J'avet's face.

"I'm sure you would have preferred to stay and blow up every Iri in the area," I said. "But a one guy rescue mission wouldn't have turned out very well."

"No." He averted his face. "Neither will a full on attack by the IF."

I frowned, trying to figure out what he meant. After a moment, it clicked in my brain.

"You think they let you escape, hoping you'd get to IF space and rouse an army?" The Iri did have a way of letting people live, if it served their own purpose.

"All those Freytauri would turn into hosts. All the metal on the ships. They'd be unstoppable."

His words made my blood run cold.

"That's why we can't go back with an armada," J'avet said. "We need stealth."

I blinked. "You just said *we*."

"Did I?" he asked, as if he didn't realise. "You understand the situation. You're human. Brinley too. That makes you immune to nanobots. Nothing we saw suggests they've solved that puzzle yet. Slek managed to access their database for a short time. So far, they can only turn Freytauri into hosts. They..." He hesitated. "They're focusing on turning Agusians. Slek thought they were close."

"Shit," I muttered. If they'd made Slek, Danec and Zarex into mindless hosts, then what would I do?

I knew what I *wouldn't* do. I wouldn't panic. That wouldn't help anyone, especially me. I would be cool and calm. Save my fury for the Iri.

"You're taking this surprisingly well," J'avet remarked.

"Would you prefer I throw myself on the floor and kick and scream?" I asked sweetly.

He smiled again, still just slightly. "No, but it seems more in character for you."

I regarded him for a moment. "If I didn't know better, I might think you're teasing."

His eyebrows twitched. "I don't tease."

"Of course you don't." I didn't believe that. Nothing he said contained malice. "You must have taken quite the hit to the head. You're almost being nice."

"I'll work on that some more," he said.

I took his empty soup bowl and handed him a cup of water with ice floating in it.

He nodded in thanks and sipped slowly.

"So when are we going?" I asked. "You should heal first. Maybe just Brinley and I should—"

He cut me off. "No. I'm not letting the two of you go by yourselves. I shudder to think of the trouble you'd get yourselves into."

"Wow," I said slowly. "It's almost as if you care."

He gave me a 'yeah, right' expression, but his eyes said something more.

Perhaps lust wasn't a one way street. How about that?

"I suppose it would be difficult with two," I said. Not that I was going to let him tell me what to do, but I was a nurse, not a soldier, pilot or a navigator… "*Chimera* is a bit big for us anyway. It would feel too empty."

"We're not taking *Chimera*," J'avet said. "She's too noticeable and too damaged. We'll take one of the pods."

I sat back and stared at him. "You mean one of the pods designed for short trips? Like, a few hundred kilometres and then they run out of fuel? Those pods?"

"We'll take spare fuel," he said evenly. "It will only be three of us."

I shook my head. "Now I *know* you're trying to get me killed."

His smile was wider this time. "Only as much as you seem to be."

I snorted. "I am never trying to get myself killed," I said firmly. "Trouble finds me wherever I go."

"Only since you left Earth," he reminded me.

"That old argument." I waved a hand. "You need to make up your mind. Do you want me to help, or go home?"

"Both," he said. "You'd be safe on Earth, but this mission is vital to the whole IF."

"No pressure then," I said.

"Not at all," he replied with a gusty sigh out his nose. "You don't even have to come. There are other humans…"

"I'm going," I said firmly. "Brinley will too."

I missed Zarex and Slek. Both would have thrown in several innuendos by now. Danec would have his bags neatly packed and ready. Within the hour we'd be out the door, so to speak.

"Was… was there any sign of Danec?" I asked gingerly.

"He wasn't one of the ones who attacked us," J'avet said. "We never saw him. I have no reason to assume he's anything but alive and deep inside the Iri compound on Tarathu."

"That's something, I suppose." I hoped the part

of him that was him, was still there. How long did it take before the host gave up fighting and surrendered to a life full of nanobots? Did that ever happen? I didn't know. I couldn't count out the idea he was gone forever, but I wouldn't give up on him until I knew for sure. Who was I kidding? Even then, I still wouldn't give up. He was mine and I was his. I would get him back, whatever it took.

"If Slek is a host, that will be more problematic," J'avet said. "His skills are ones we need. He taught me a lot about the things he did to disable the nanobots, but if they've evolved, then..."

"We'll deal with it," I said firmly. I didn't want to think about Slek as an Iri either. He would hate it even more than Danec. Slek was a free spirit, in every sense of the word. His engineering abilities, in the hands of the Iri, I didn't bear thinking about either. The only reason I did was that, from what I had seen, the nanobots, or whoever programmed them, did the thinking. The hosts were just bodies. In that case, they couldn't make use of Slek's skills, unless the head asshole accessed them.

"Is there anyone else we could trust, who could help?" I asked.

J'avet put a hand to his head, as though to scratch

near the wound. His frown when he touched the hardened healing substance almost made me laugh.

He gave me a dry look and lowered his hand. "I'm sure you understand by now I don't trust very many, very often," he said.

"No shit," I replied. "Is that a no?"

"I know a man," he said, as though he hadn't heard my question. "Another Parvoran. You met him on board *Infinity*."

I scrunched up my brow and thought. "The guy who was with you when you told me I was too dumb to play chess?"

"The same." J'avet didn't look even slightly sorry for the things he'd said that day. "E'rel doesn't have the ability or imagination Slek does, but he'll be adequate."

"High praise," I said sarcastically. "What do you say about people you actually like?"

"I tell them they should go somewhere safe," he said.

It took me a moment to grasp his meaning. When I did, I snapped my fingers. "I *knew* you were hot for me. Too hard to admit it, hmmm?" I glanced at his groin to emphasise the double meaning.

"I'm getting tired," J'avet said. "You're exhausting."

Rather than being offended, I smiled. "I've heard

that. In the best way possible though."

He smirked. "Keep telling yourself that." The grumpyass was back, but I thought we'd reached a new understanding. One in which we didn't hate each other. I would call that progress.

"Do you want me to talk to E'rel?" I asked. I had seen him around the station. He'd always looked like he was avoiding me, but truthfully I hadn't given it, or him, much thought. Any friend of J'avet's was unlikely to be a friend of mine. Until now.

"No, I will," J'avet said. "He'll have as much patience for you as I do. I don't want him to give an outright no because you irritate him."

"If that's his attitude, this is going to be a long journey," I said with a sigh.

"You can still say no," J'avet said.

"And miss all the fun? Not a chance." I took his cup and placed it on the table beside his bed. "If I can put up with you, then I can put up with two assholes."

There was that faint smile again. "Are all humans so stubborn?" he asked.

"Are all Parvorans?" I asked in response. "Is it true all your women stay home on Parvora while the men go out to space?"

J'avet grimaced. "On Parvora, space travel is

considered a lesser activity. Most women wouldn't lower themselves to try it. Some do. Most do not."

I frowned. "So if you go home, you're looked down upon?"

"I would be, but I don't go home," he replied.

My mouth formed an O. He looked so sad I almost wanted to cry for him.

"That explains why you're cranky all the time," I said. "Bitter and twisted from being treated so badly. But then, in turn, you treated me like crap."

"I was just being honest," he said, but I sensed he knew he was running out of wiggle room here.

"Sure." I drew out the word. "You mean you want to keep people at arm's length, so they don't do anything horrible to you. You put up walls as high as the galaxy."

"And you cannot respect my desire to keep people on the other side of that wall," he stated.

"Nope," I replied easily. "No one should be stuck behind a fortress. It's not healthy."

"You're a psychiatrist now?" he asked.

"No, I have common sense." I ignored his snort and added, "Everyone needs to have someone care about them. It would be a lonely life without that."

I knew that all too well. The past month, if it wasn't for Brinley, I would have been lonely as hells.

5

"FOR THE RECORD, you should be resting," I told J'avet. "I'm mentioning it in case later someone thinks you weren't told."

"Noted," J'avet said. "Consider your ass covered."

"Hey," I protested. "I'm not *just* trying to cover my ass." I also knew he wouldn't listen anyway, even if I insisted.

"Did you say it because you care?" He glanced at me over his shoulder.

"Hells no," I said lightly. "You're still an asshole." I placed another can of food into the locker at the side of the pod.

"Glad we cleared that up." He went back to tapping at the pod controls.

I turned back and frowned at the back of his

head for a while. The doctor had removed the healing shell that morning, and murmured sounds of approval.

"Come back each day so I can check your progress." Barek gave J'avet a nod and moved away, to see another patient.

Apparently J'avet took that as permission to leave the station after only two days.

"The doctor is going to be pissed," I pointed out. I closed the locker door, leaned against it and crossed my arms.

"You surprise me." J'avet glanced up. "I thought you would be the one pushing to leave."

I shifted from foot to foot. "The sooner we go, the better. But if you drop dead from that head wound, you'll be no use to us, or the others." That included the whole crew of the *Chimera*, not just the guys. A few hundred of various species, although only two apart from Slek were Freytauri.

"Then it's your job to make sure that doesn't happen," he concluded.

"I can check your wound, but you're not going to listen when I tell you to rest." I cocked my head and gave him a challenging look.

He smirked. "Of course not. I haven't listened to you yet. Why would I start now?"

I shook my head. "You're such an ass."

"You're such a pain in my neck," he retorted.

"It's not my fault you can't recognise awesomeness when you see it," I joked.

"Of course I can," he said. He looked so smug I wanted to sock his arm.

"Well then," I said with a sniff. "You could show more appreciation for it."

He shook his head and stood. For a moment I thought he was leaving the pod. Instead, he moved like a flash of lightning.

Before I could take a breath, he had me pressed against the locker with the full length of his body. His nose was a finger width from mine. His breath brushed my lips.

"Is this what you had in mind?" He curled his fingers in my hair and pressed his mouth hard against mine.

I could only respond with a moan. I had imagined what it would be like to kiss him, but this was more than I could have expected. His lips were firm, demanding, like a lifetime of pent up desire that needed release.

His tongue traced my lips and slipped inside my mouth when I opened for him.

He broke off the kiss, gave me a scorching look

and moved back into trail heated kisses down my cheek and neck.

"Edie," he said, his mouth muffled by my skin. "I want you."

"Mmm. I want you too." As frustrating as he was, the attraction was undeniable. The guys had all given me their permission to explore relationships with other guys, including each other and J'avet. Zarex, in particular, encouraged it. He always said he couldn't fulfil all my needs, so I should have more guys in my life to cover every angle, so to speak.

J'avet—well, he gave me a challenge. I never knew what he would do or say next. Someday I might have to choose a guy, but we had to get the others back first.

J'avet slid a hand under my shirt and ran it lightly over the front of my bra. Through the fabric, he pinched my nipple.

I twitched, but made no effort to pull away. The slight sensation of pain drove a knot of arousal right to my core.

His hand was still in my hair while the other started on working down the zipper on the front of my shirt. Lucky I hadn't put on the one with a bajil-lion buttons on the front this morning.

I slipped out of my shirt and somehow my bra

joined it a moment later. Evidently J'avet was better with those than Slek. I hadn't even felt him unhook it.

My pants went next, then my panties, until I was naked and J'avet was still fully dressed.

"Your turn," I said. I helped him with his shirt, then leaned my head back to get a good look. He was as muscular as the other guys. Every bit of him was covered in the same fine fur as his face, but it did nothing to hide the definition of his abs, or his biceps. His stomach was flat and smooth, down to the V of his hips. Those disappeared into his pants until I pushed down the zipper and worked them off.

They were the same type of underpants he'd worn in the infirmary. At least until he tugged them down and out of the way.

I blinked at the expanse of smoothness at his groin. He had a plate of bone, like an eyelid across his pubic area.

"So," I drew the word out, "how does this work?"

He smiled and the plate of bone slid up, retracting into his belly as though it had never been.

Gingerly, I put out a hand, but I could barely feel where it had gone. Only a hint of something hard, as long as my hand, gave any sign of it.

"That's amazing," I marvelled. Also pretty amazing was the erect cock which had hidden under the plate. "How the hells did you fit that under there?"

For the first time since I'd met him, he grinned.

"Just one of those things." He gripped my hair tighter and jerked my head back so he could kiss my neck again.

His other hand, he dipped between my legs. With slow, firm strokes, he rubbed at my clit and entrance with his whole hand.

I moaned and started to buck against his hand.

He pushed one of my legs aside more and pressed his hand inside me. No finger-at-a-time, for him. No, he shoved in every finger and he shoved it hard.

"You're so warm, so wet already," he said, as if he talked about the weather.

"I try," I said breathlessly.

Before I could say another word, he yanked his hand out and turned me away from him. He pushed me forward until my upper body lay over the nearest console. His hand tight in my hair, he guided his cock to my entrance and slammed into me.

I gasped out loud at the sudden, almost violent penetration. He was big too, bigger than Slek. When he pounded harder and harder, I was sure he'd split me in two.

He groaned with the effort and slammed into me deeper, until each thrust filled me with delicious pain.

"J'avet," I said breathlessly. I drew closer and closer to coming, but not over the edge. Whatever he was doing, somehow it wouldn't quite let me orgasm. I was on the brink one moment and back from the brink in another. Then on the brink again.

He grunted and tugged on my hair until I had to throw my head back to keep him from tearing out my curls. He was definitely the one in charge here. Strangely, I didn't mind letting go, letting him do whatever he wanted to my body.

He slowed a little and his spare hand snaked around to pinch my nipple again. He gripped it and twisted so hard I cried out in pain and pleasure.

That drove him harder and faster than ever.

He squeezed my nipple so tight tears sprang to my eyes. That was what it took to drive me all the way over the edge, into the most intense, powerful orgasm I'd ever had. I was lost in a whirlpool of pleasure that sucked me in, held me under and turned me every which way.

A trickle of water made it last even longer. Or

maybe I came again. It was so close to the first time, I couldn't tell. It didn't matter.

J'avet moaned and ground into me as he came too. His wet heat flooded my pussy. His moans flooded the rest of me, every nerve in my body tingling with a mixture of my pleasure and his.

Then he sagged against my back and finally let go of my hair.

We panted in unison while we came down from the rush we gave each other. After a hundred life-times, he pulled his cock out of me. Although I ached, my pussy immediately missed him.

There will be other times, I told myself.

"We should consider the sleeping arrangements on this journey," J'avet said in my ear. He put his hand lightly around the front of my neck and pulled me off the console.

"Yeah," I said, still trying to catch my breath. "I want to do that again. Unless you snore."

I felt his chest rumble in response.

"You're insufferable," he said, but this time there was a touch of affection in his tone.

"You too," I retorted. "What did I say about resting?"

His chest shook now and I caught the sound of him chuckling softly.

"You said I should rest, then you led me astray. This is definitely your fault."

"Fuck off," I said, before I realised he was teasing. I twisted around until I was face to face with him, my ass hard against the console. "We should get washed up."

He dipped his head to kiss me lightly on the mouth.

"Yes, we should. E'rel and Brinley will be here soon."

My eyes widened. I had totally forgotten about them. They could easily have walked in on us. They still might.

"I call first dibs on checking out the pod's shower." I slid out from between him and the console, and bent to gather up my clothes.

He pinched my ass and made me jump.

"Hey!" I stood up straight just as his pubic plate slid back into place. "Not fair, I can't knee you in the groin now. Not without hurting my kneecap."

He looked unapologetic. "Why do you think I have that?" He nodded downward.

"Dirty cheat," I muttered, but I grinned. "Shame there's only room in the shower for one person at a time." I could barely lift my arms, much less share.

He shrugged and started to pull his clothes on. "Don't use up all the water."

"It gets recycled, smartass," I told him. Unless someone stole the water, as the Iri presumably had with the *Chimera*, then we'd never run out. It might taste a little stale after a while, but it would keep us alive and clean.

He arched an eyebrow at me and turned away. Just like the usual, grumpy old J'avet. Frustrating bastard.

I watched him slip back into the chair behind the console before I heard a voice outside. I bit back a squeak of alarm and hurried into the tiny bathroom before Brinley or E'rel stepped aboard.

They might wonder at my timing—having a shower in the middle of the day. Let them wonder. They'd figure out what was going on soon enough. I just hoped I could figure it out first. Was this just attraction and lust, or the start of something more? Hells, we had to go into the heart of the enemy, get the others out and escape with our lives, before we could even think about romance.

I dumped my clothes on a small shelf and stepped into water slightly too hot for comfort. I would need every muscle relaxant I could get after that session.

6

I MIGHT AS WELL HAVE PARADED AROUND naked. Brinley took one look at me and grinned.

E'rel barely glanced in my direction before he slid into a seat in the cockpit.

Brinley swung her bag onto a bunk and raised an eyebrow at me.

"What?" I asked. I started to arrange the new box of cans E'rel had brought on board and left near the door.

Acting like an ass wasn't just a Parvoran thing, but they did it so well. They could teach the average politician a trick or two.

"You know what." She picked up her pillow and made a face at how thin it was. "You and J'avet."

I shrugged, although my face suddenly felt

warmer. "Just two consenting adults doing what adults do."

She snapped her fingers. "I knew you two didn't hate each other. It was so obvious."

"Apparently to everyone but us," I said. "Who said we don't still hate each other? He's still an ass."

J'avet stepped aboard, bag over one shoulder, yet another box of cans in his arms.

"Don't forget it either," he said dryly. "Don't start thinking I'll be nice."

"I wouldn't dream of it," I told him. "What did you say to Vaw? I don't think it's gone unnoticed that we're stocking this pod."

"Officially, we're meeting up with the *Vulcan*," J'avet said. "That will take us to Agus."

I narrowed my eyes. That sounded so plausible, I wouldn't put it past him to plan just that.

"But we're not, right?" I asked. I expected him to hesitate, to avert his eyes. Instead, he looked straight at me.

"No. We're not. Unless you've changed your mind and still want to—"

"I haven't," I said firmly. Okay, a small part of me would have liked to run away to Agus, but I had a month to do that. Honestly, I never really thought about it as a viable option. For so long, I figured the guys would turn up. Now, they needed me. There was nowhere else in the galaxy I would be but here. Okay, maybe a larger ship, with a metric butt load of experienced, heavily armed soldiers.

J'avet turned to Brinley. "There are other pilots."

"I'm going," she said firmly. "Wherever Edie goes, I go."

"I wouldn't make that a hard and fast rule if I were you," J'avet placed his bag on the bunk above mine. "Edie doesn't always make the best choices."

I sniffed. "Ain't that the truth." I looked at him down my lashes and held back a smile.

"Very much so," he agreed. "We'll be lucky to get out of this alive." He left the box of cans at my feet and went to sit beside E'rel.

"See," I said, "he's still an ass."

"So I see." Brinley looked like she was holding back laughter. She patted me on the shoulder and moved to sit in the pilot's seat to start the preflight check.

Muttering to myself, I went on unpacking cans until the lockers were full and boxes were empty. I carried the empty boxes off the shuttle and put them beside the docking bay door in a neat pile.

Many people left them lying around, but I

figured this would make life easier for the station's maintenance people.

Of course it also made me anxious that J'avet would close the pod door and leave without me. To my relief, the door was still open when I got back.

I took a last glance around the pod bay, then stepped up the gangway and into the pod. Who knew if we would ever be back? Even if we survived this crazy mission, we might not come this way again.

Part of me was sad about that. As stations went, this was a nice place to spend a few weeks. The rest of me got stir crazy after the first day, and couldn't wait to leave.

I pressed my hand against the palm pad. When it flashed green, I pressed the button to close the door. I half expected to see a contingent of security officers come running to stop us from essentially stealing a pod.

No one came. I guess J'avet's story and rank was enough to convince them we weren't up to something.

"I'm inputting the coordinates to the rendezvous site," Brinley said over the pod's comm system.

"You're cleared for departure," a voice said in reply. "Safe travels."

"Thank you," Brinley said brightly. She turned off the comms and pressed a few of the buttons in front of her. The pod hummed and lifted up a couple of handspans above the docking bay deck.

"As soon as we're clear, I'll modify the coordinates," she said. "We're going to have to travel a hundred kilometres in the wrong direction first though."

"It can't be helped," J'avet said. "I'd prefer not to waste fuel, but they'll send a ship after us if we head right for Iri space. The pod can't outrun anything except another pod."

"That's a cheery thought." I leaned against the cockpit door and crossed my arms. "If the Iri come after us—"

"I have a plan," J'avet said.

"Care to share?" I asked.

"Perhaps you could allow the pilot to concentrate," E'rel suggested coldly.

I regarded him for a moment, then smiled. "That's Parvoran for 'you like Brinley.' How adorable."

He twisted around to give me a dirty look, but J'avet seemed amused.

"I'm merely suggesting you be quiet," E'rel said before he turned away.

"Sure." I nodded. "I'm happy for you both. You'll be adorable together." They really would.

Brinley looked back at me and gave me a wink. So she felt it too, hmmm?

Wait, why did I suddenly get the feeling this wasn't a new thing? I had been somewhat distracted for the last few weeks. They could have been seeing each other for ages and I hadn't noticed. I made a mental note to ask Brinley for the details later. In the meantime, I felt like a pretty crap friend for not seeing this sooner. Talk about being self absorbed.

I was dragged from my thoughts by the opening of the docking bay doors. We passed through them, into the airlock and out into space.

I don't think I would ever be tired of looking at the open expanse of space spread out in front of us. Stars upon stars twinkled like fairy lights. A small fraction of what I saw out the window was IF space. Beyond that were more unexplored galaxies than a person could count. I knew the IF planned to send their people out there some day, when technology advanced more.

Personally, I had only seen a small portion of the galaxy. When this was over, I wanted to see more. Frey-T, Parvora, not to mention Agus. It felt like years since I left Earth, headed straight for there.

'Straight' turned into a wiggly line, with a few loops thrown in.

I sighed and moved into the main sitting space of the pod. From here, I got a good view of the station disappearing behind us.

"Undapan Station to Commander J'avet." The voice startled me. My heart began to race.

J'avet looked uncertain for a moment, but opened the comms. "Commander J'avet here."

"You are requested to return to the station immediately," the voice said. "Doctor Barek has not cleared you for travel."

J'avet turned his face enough that I saw him grimace. He looked back toward the comm panel. "I feel fine," he said firmly. "I have a nurse with me to see to my needs."

I scowled at the back of his head. His needs? He made me sound like a servant.

"You didn't clear this mission with Doctor Barek?" I asked.

J'avet glanced over his shoulder. "He would have said no."

I shook my head. "You're such a rebel." I was going to be in a world of trouble now, aiding him in his escape from the station.

"We didn't have time to waste." J'avet ran a hand over his head and winced as he touched the wound.

"Commander, you're ordered to return to the station until further notice. Failure to comply may result in disciplinary action."

"When you put it that way," J'avet said. He turned off the comms. "You might as well change those coordinates now. They're going to come after us no matter what we do."

Brinley nodded, keyed in the change and pushed the pod to move faster.

"Commander, we've detected an unauthorised course change." The station couldn't hear us, but we could hear them well enough.

J'avet sighed and turned the comms back on. "Yes, we seem to be experiencing some trouble with navigation. We—"

I stepped forward and held my fingers in front of his face, slightly apart.

J'avet frowned, then nodded. "Undapan Station, I think we have nanobots on board. They're... taking over the pod. We have no control over..." He turned off the comms again and sat back.

"There. That should keep them off our backs for a moment," he said.

"Unless they decide to blow us up." E'rel looked unimpressed.

"Blowing us up won't kill the bots," Brinley said.

"*Chimera* is the only ship currently on the station which is equipped with a laser," J'avet said. "And she's out of commission for a while." He looked smug.

I regarded him for a moment. "J'avet. Did you sabotage the *Chimera*?"

He smirked. "Just enough to give us time to get away."

"You really are a rebel," I said, impressed.

"I also commandeered some devices Slek made that could help us."

I waited for him to elaborate, but he didn't. "I'll go and keep an eye on the station. They might send someone after us anyway."

J'avet nodded. He looked weary. That wasn't surprising. He'd been beaten up, injured and left more or less for dead, with no food or water. If it was me, I would want to rest for a year.

I ran a hand over my hair and wondered if I should insist we turn back. If J'avet died because he was away from a doctor's care for too long... I sucked in a breath and reminded myself that, barring further injury, there wasn't anything a doctor could do that I couldn't do as well.

I plopped into a seat and watched the station out the window. For a while, I actually thought they'd let us go.

Naive, right? I know. This mission was important. If we succeeded, the whole IF would thank us. After they tossed us in the brig for a few years and threw us out of our jobs.

When they figured out what we'd done, they'd appreciate us, right?

A speck of black appeared in the side of the station. At first I thought I was seeing things. I blinked a few times and focused my eyes. Nope, it was definitely there and getting bigger by the moment.

"The docking bay doors are opening!" I called out. "There's a ship coming through."

E'rel brought up the rear camera and put the vision on a screen at the back of the pod.

"You couldn't do that before?" I muttered. It would have saved my eyes.

He said nothing.

"It's the *Gamma*," Brinley said. "They aren't messing around."

"That sounds bad," I said.

"She's a small vessel, but fast," Brinley said. "Equipped with sonic canons and—" She listed a bunch of features which meant nothing to me, but sounded like a galaxy of pain.

"We can't outrun her," J'avet said.

"Especially if she's come to blow the shit out of us," I said.

"Especially then," he agreed. He rubbed his hand over his forehead.

He looked so defeated, all I could do was watch the screen.

I guess this was the time to kiss my ass goodbye.

Shit. I *really* had not planned to die today.

I pressed my lips together and watched the *Gamma* draw closer.

7

"This might be a good time to let them know we don't have any nanobots on board," Brinley said.

E'rel and J'avet both turned and scowled at me, as though it was my fault for making the suggestion in the first place.

I scowled back. "You didn't have to tell them that. You could have ignored me like you usually do."

The side of J'avet's mouth twitched upward. I couldn't tell if he was apologetic or thinking he should stick to ignoring me.

Either way, he turned away and opened the comms again.

"*Gamma*, this is Commander J'avet. We were mistaken about the presence of nanobots on board. My apologies. Stand down."

He sounded so firm I would have done what he told me to do. Maybe. Depending on what it was.

The *Gamma* took a while to respond. When they did, it was a female voice which spoke.

"Commander J'avet, that is what I would expect the Iritauri to say."

I suppressed a snort, which ended up as a cough. She had us there.

"I'll turn on the vidscreen," J'avet said. "You'll see two humans and two Parvorans." He pressed a button and a light turned on, right in my eyes.

I waved and smiled at the camera. It didn't hurt to look friendly.

"Captain Vaw has ordered your return to the station." The vidscreen went both ways. The woman who spoke was also human, to my surprise, with an insignia which marked her as captain of the *Gamma*.

J'avet nodded curtly. "I'm fine," he said. "We have an important mission to carry out. We can't delay any longer, not even for my health."

I'm pretty sure *Gamma's* captain matched my eyebrow rise at the arrogance in his tone. He was right though. Not even for him could we turn back.

"If you think the whole station doesn't know you're headed back to Iritauri space, then think again," she said dryly. "Your organisation didn't go unnoticed."

J'avet swore under his breath.

I moved to stand behind him. "Why let us go then?" I asked.

"Because we need you to go," she replied. "This way, it doesn't involve Captain Vaw, or anyone else in the IF. We can all turn a blind eye, having made an effort to order you to turn back."

"Should you be telling us this?" I asked.

She smiled. "Probably not, but I'll have this recording deleted when we're finished. Officially, we fired a warning shot, but you evaded us."

"Warning shot?" Brinley asked.

Light flashed from the front of *Gamma* and something blasted over our heads, close enough to rock the whole pod.

The only one standing, I was knocked off my feet and thrown hard into the far wall. Tears of pain sprang to my eyes.

"Edie!" Brinley called out.

I struggled to my feet and rubbed my shoulder where I'd hit. Nothing was broken, but I would have a nasty bruise to show for it.

"I'm okay," I said, glaring at the screen where *Gamma's* captain looked unapologetic.

"Lucky for you, it was only a warning," she said coolly.

I was tempted to tell her to fuck right off, but she might change her mind about letting us go.

J'avet looked furious and his face was redder than ever. That was saying something, since he was red anyway.

I got another surprise when he said, "You could escort us part of the way there."

E'rel scowled at him. I was starting to realise that was his default expression in response to everything. He was even less cheerful than J'avet.

I'd probably be pissed too if my whole planet treated me like I was a lesser being, just because I wanted to go to space.

"It would save fuel if we spent some of the journey in their pod bay," Brinley said.

J'avet gave the smallest of nods. The corners of his eyes crinkled as though he was in pain. When had he taken pain relief last?

I glanced at my watch. Long enough. He was due for more.

"*Gamma* does have an infirmary," I said. "That would satisfy Doctor Barek. We might not even get in too much trouble when we get back." Maybe.

If we get back. There was always a chance we wouldn't. Okay, a *big* chance.

"Thanks for the offer," *Gamma's* captain said, "But I prefer not to be court martialed."

"Scared to take *Gamma* near Iri space?" J'avet asked, his chin raised in challenge.

"That too," she agreed. "Now hurry up and evade me before I change my mind."

"Evading," Brinley confirmed. "Edie, buckle up."

I hurried to do as she said. I'd witnessed enough for her evasive flying to know I might get thrown around again.

Hard pass.

"Good luck," *Gamma's* captain said before the screen went black.

"We'll need it," I muttered.

"Any damage from her warning shot?" J'avet addressed the question to E'rel.

The other Parvoran shook his head. "No. It was calculated to rattle the pod, not do us any harm."

I rubbed my shoulder again. "She did us some harm," I pointed out.

"Any *significant* harm," E'rel said without looking at me.

J'avet glanced back and gave me a questioning look. He actually seemed worried.

Well of course he did, we both knew he cared about me, even if he wouldn't let on too much.

"I'm fine," I said. "Just bruised. Nothing broken."

His mouth turned up at the corners in the tiniest of smiles.

"Good. Stay belted in until we're clear of the station, and *Gamma*." Something in his eyes suggested he'd like to see me restrained for a while longer, and not in a pod harness. Okay, maybe in a pod harness, but not with clothes on.

I smiled knowingly. "I'm not going anywhere," I told him. "Except to get you painkillers when we're clear. And to make you lie down."

"I could use a lie down," he said.

"Alone," I added.

He scowled, but I was used to him by now and just smiled again.

"You can't help anyone if you're dead," I pointed out.

"She's right, you know," Brinley said. "Also, I think the *Gamma* is following us. They've dropped back to make it look like they aren't, but they are."

As long as they didn't fire anymore warning shots, it would be nice to know they lurked back there. We might need them before we got to Iri space, especially if J'avet argued with me about resting. As important as this mission was, I wouldn't hesitate to call them and make him—okay, *try* to make him—go to their infirmary and rest.

"So, Vaw knew about this the entire time," I said conversationally. "That explains a lot. Like, why no one seemed to mind us taking so many cans. And why this seemed so much easier than it should have been."

"And why no one stopped me from taking a drum or two of fuel," Brinley said. "More than we would need to rendezvous with the *Vulcan*."

"We could have avoided a lot of sneaking around," I said with a sigh.

"The sneaking around was kind of fun," Brinley said. She smiled at E'rel before returning her attention to the ship's controls.

E'rel's face turned darker, which I interpreted as a blush.

"Yeah, well no sneaking now," I said. "We'll have to do our best to keep out of each other's way." In a ship smaller than an inner city apartment in most cities on Earth. Yeah, right. We'd be lucky if we didn't throttle each other halfway there.

"Two take the day shift, two take the night," J'avet said simply.

"That works," I said. As long as I wasn't on the

same shift as E'rel. One cranky Parvoran was enough. J'avet I could handle, more or less. E'rel, well, I'd leave him to Brinley.

"I should get to work," E'rel said. "These devices that Freytaurian gave you are crude at best."

"I hope you're not referring to Slek as 'that Freytaurian', are you?" I asked, my hackles immediately up.

E'rel rose, gave me a glance and moved to the back of the pod.

"Well, he's charming," I muttered sarcastically.

"Don't mind him," Brinley said. "He's better with machines than people. It takes him a while to get comfortable with someone."

"Sounds familiar." I looked pointedly at J'avet. "Speaking of you, it's time you rested. And don't even try to argue, or the three of us will drag you onto a bunk and tie you down."

Slek would have asked, "Do you promise?" but J'avet just looked resigned. He touched his head lightly and winced.

"I could use something for this," he admitted. At least he was man enough to know when he'd reached his limit. I wasn't sure the other three did. Not to mention every other guy in the history of guys. Okay, I'm exaggerating, but I'm a nurse. I've seen it over and over again for years. People hate to admit they're hurt, no matter what species they are. The fact J'avet could admit it made me respect him more.

Although, the fact he said anything might also mean he was in a lot more pain than he let on.

"Come on then." I jerked my head toward the bunk room. "I'll tuck you in."

"Is that what they're calling that now?" Brinley asked teasingly.

I stuck my tongue out at her and stepped back to let J'avet out of the cockpit.

"I'm starting to think you should have been lying down since before we left the station." I clicked my tongue at him.

"Someone needed to deal with Captain Marshall," he said.

"Was that her name? Oh, is that Jenny Marshall? I've heard people complaining about her. She takes no shit from anyone."

He gave me a lopsided half smile, half grimace. "Like you."

"Exactly." I followed him into the bunk room and helped him pull his shirt carefully off over his head.

From the look on his face, even that much effort took a lot out of him.

"I really should have left you back at the station." He sat while I got out some pain relief.

"I would have followed you," he growled. "Without me, you would have gotten yourself killed by now."

"I would not," I protested. "Give me some credit. I'd last at least a full day out here." Probably a bit more, but I would humour him if it kept him still while I checked his wound. It was healing nicely, but not as nicely as it would have if he'd rested.

I applied some healing salve and gave him an injection of pain relief which would work better on him than good, old fashioned tablets like humans prefer to pop.

Before we left, I'd scoured the medical database for information on Parvoran physiology. I'd down-loaded it to a tablet, then to the ship, but I'd read as much as I was able to. I needed as much knowledge in my brain as I could get. If he started to crash, I wouldn't have time to consult a computer.

"Okay, lie back," I said. I plumped his flat pillow a couple of times before he placed his head on it.

"Hey, that's a first," I said.

He eyed me. "What is?"

"You did what I told you to," I said with a grin.

He snorted. "Don't get used to it. You're still a pain in my ass, like all humans."

I sniffed and pretended to be offended. "I'll have you know, us humans are awesome."

He brushed a soft, lightly furred hand over my cheek. "Yes, you are. You and Brinley, at least. The rest I've met, I could live without."

"You say that, until the *Gamma* saves our asses," I said. "I think you'll be happy to see Captain Marshall then."

"Possibly." He brushed his thumb over my lips.

"You should sleep," I said.

"Only if you lie next to me." He scooted over to the wall.

"There's barely room for two sticks of dried spaghetti," I said. In spite of that, I lay down in the small space left and lay facing him. It was a tight squeeze, but comfortable enough.

He placed a hand on my hip and closed his eyes. For a long time, I watched him sleep, then I drifted off myself.

8

"THAT CAN'T BE GOOD," Brinley said.

"What can't be good?" I asked. That sentence was right up there with 'we need to talk' for sending shivers down my spine.

I know, priorities, right? An awkward conversation is so much worse than an emergency in space.

Brinley scratched the side of her head.

J'avet moved to stand behind me, his hand lightly on my shoulder.

"What is it?" he asked, even though he could read the controls as well as she could.

I glanced back to take in his expression, but he gave nothing away. At least he didn't seem panicked. If anything did that to him, it would probably be too late for us all.

"*Gamma* to rogue pod." Captain Marshall's voice came through the speakers and made me jump. "I presume you've seen the ship approaching on a course to intercept you."

Brinley looked to J'avet questioningly.

He nodded.

She opened a comm channel, without visuals for now.

That was lucky, my hair looked like a bird had tried to make a nest in it, but gave up because it was too messy.

After all these years, they still hadn't developed the technology to permanently tame curly hair. If they put as much effort into that as they did making nanobots, they'd have a solution by now. Never mind the fact the nanobots were created by Freytaurians and none of them had curly hair. Surely someone could have had the foresight...

I gave myself a mental head shake.

Ship?

Shit.

"We saw, Captain," Brinley said. "We can't tell from here if they're IF or Iritauri."

"Have you tried to contact them?" J'avet asked bluntly.

"Not yet," Marshall replied. "Just checking if you wanted to do the honours."

"If it's Iritauri, I would prefer to stay out of their way," J'avet said.

"I thought you might," Marshall replied. "I'll have a little chat with them. *Gamma* out." The comms went silent.

"They aren't going to do what I think they're going to do, are they?" I asked.

"I think that depends on what you think they'll do," Brinley said.

"You know me, I have a wild imagination," I said. *And damn, J'avet is massaging my shoulder.*

"We'll have to wait and see," J'avet said. "Prepare to evade the incoming ship, in case it's necessary."

Brinley nodded. "I've already plotted an alternate course."

That explained why she was tapping buttons the moment she mentioned the ship.

J'avet nodded. "Good." He said nothing else, but I felt his tension in the way he dug his fingers in slightly too hard.

I flinched. "Ouch."

He didn't apologise, but he did lighten up.

The comms buzzed before Marshall spoke again.

"They didn't respond. I made them an offer to

leave IF space before I fire on them. You'll note their change of course."

"They're heading toward the *Gamma*," Brinley said.

"Change course," J'avet said. "Take us away from both ships."

"Getting the hells out of here so we don't end up as a ship sandwich," Brinley said with a nod.

"Definitely the worst kind of sandwich," I agreed.

"I don't think a laser sandwich sounds like much fun," Brinley remarked.

I grinned.

"No, but a canon sandwich—"

"I see being annoying is a human thing," J'avet said dryly.

"I don't think so," I replied. "I think it's universal. You're pretty annoying too." I gave him a smile over my shoulder.

The side of his mouth twitched. "I don't think you can make a comparison between us."

"That's true," I replied. "I'm nowhere near as annoying as you."

Brinley stifled a laugh.

"You're all equally irritating," E'rel said. He looked as though he'd just woken up.

"Did we wake you?" Brinley sounded genuinely concerned.

His scowl softened slightly when he looked at her. Yeah, he had it really bad.

"I should have woken an hour ago," he said. His scowl was back in place again.

"You were sleeping so peacefully, I thought I'd let you sleep for a while longer," Brinley said.

I exchanged glances with J'avet. If he also thought they were too cute for words, he gave no indication. His expression gave me no hint as to what he was thinking.

"Next time, don't let me oversleep," E'rel snapped. He turned and stalked back toward his corner to work on various gadgets, or whatever he did back there.

Halfway there, he stopped, and turned his face back to say, "Please."

Brinley nodded, although she looked unimpressed.

If he was interested in her, he was going to have to work harder than that. J'avet, for all his flaws, at least displayed moments of reasonable, compassionate behaviour. He was frustrating and confusing, but I knew there was someone decent in there. More or less. When I didn't want to kick his ass. Which was often, but it went both ways. Sometimes I even deserved it, but not often.

"The unidentified ship is almost in visual range," Brinley said. "I'll turn on the screen when it is." To me, she added, "Having screens running uses more fuel."

"That makes sense," I said. "Don't want to end up with a flat battery."

"Not out here," she agreed. "And not right now. That would be bad."

"There's *Gamma*," J'avet said.

The ship soared past us, at an angle so she wouldn't collide with us on the way past. For a small ship, she was enormous compared to our pod. A cruise ship beside a dinghy. A whale beside a tuna. An elephant beside… Well you get it.

"There it is." Brinley turned on the screen. At the edge was a dot. The dot was moving quickly and getting bigger by the moment. It soon became clear that whoever piloted the ship, she was a lot bigger than *Gamma*.

That made us the dot.

I peered closely at the screen. "Wait, is that…"

"It looks like it," Brinley agreed.

"*Infinity*," J'avet said.

"Wasn't she at Dendra Station, getting repaired?"

From what Slek had said, she'd be there for months. I wasn't the best at adding up, but I was almost certain it hadn't been months since we left Dendra.

"She was." J'avet looked troubled. More than I ever saw him before.

That, in turn, made me worried. "Then why—"

"I don't know," he said, cutting me off. "Brinley, can you listen in to any conversations between *Infinity* and *Gamma*?"

"Sure. If they have any. So far, I'm not picking up anything from *Infinity*."

J'avet hesitated, then nodded. He stepped back and asked, "E'rel, have you finished upgrading the Iri scanner?"

I frowned and swivelled around in my chair. Iri scanner? That sounded very much like a Slek thing. My heart ached at the idea of anyone having to work on his creations. He should be here, with his ridiculously big muscles and ready smile. The guy's heart was at least as big as the rest of him. So was his goofy side.

I swallowed down a knot of emotion. I hadn't let myself wallow, because I knew it wouldn't help anyone, but I acutely missed all of the guys right now. How in the worlds would I choose one, when I cared about them all?

I sighed loudly.

"We'll get them back," Brinley said. "Whatever it takes, okay?"

I nodded. "I know, I just wish they were all here. If they were, we'd all be somewhere else." I frowned at my own, slightly confusing logic, but it made some kind of sense.

Brinley smiled. "I know what you mean. We'd all be on Agus by now. I hear they have bathtubs."

Now we both sighed.

"Here." E'rel pushed a long, thin device toward J'avet. "You need not plug it into anything, just aim and press that button. The screen there—" he pointed, "—will show Iri signatures."

"Nice work." J'avet said.

"I merely worked from the plans I was given." E'rel shrugged and moved back to his corner.

J'avet aimed the device toward the *Infinity* and pressed the button as E'rel said.

"One… two hundred life signs," he said, distracted by his attention on the small screen. "All Iritauri."

"Fuck," I muttered.

"Yes indeed," J'avet said. "They might have missed some nanobots when they cleared out the ship."

Or they'd invaded Dendra station, and who knows where else.

He didn't say any of that, but I was sure he was thinking it.

I was.

"Um," Brinley said. "They've launched a pod. It's on a course toward us."

"Increase our speed," J'avet said. "We need to get out of here."

"The pod is equipped with a laser," E'rel said from his corner.

"And using it in sight of *Infinity* will make us a target," J'avet said.

"Putting the pedal to the metal," Brinley said.

J'avet gave her a funny look, but said nothing.

"Would you actually fire on them?" I asked. "Those on board are there against their wills. They're innocent." More or less.

"If it's them or us, I will," J'avet replied. "Until then, let's try to outrun them. There's a comet field not far from our current position."

Brinley groaned. "Comet field? Do you know how hard it is to fly through those?"

"Harder than dying?" J'avet asked dryly.

She snapped her fingers. "Good point. Okay, comet field it is. The other pod is on our tail. If we can evade them for a day or two, they'll run out of fuel. That is, if they don't start firing first."

"They must want the pod in one piece, or they would have done that by now," J'avet said thoughtfully.

"Or they want us alive," I said. "I mean, it is us."

J'avet snorted. "I can't dismiss that possibility."

"*Infinity* is firing on *Gamma*," Brinley said, her voice higher than usual. She brought the visuals up on the screen for us all to watch in silent horror.

Gamma shot back with what looked like a long laser. *Infinity* shook with the impact.

"Laser and sonic canon," Brinley said. "You can't see the cannon until it hits. When it does, it packs a punch." She sounded awed, but a little scared at the same time.

I frowned. "I thought *Gamma* didn't have lasers?" I glanced toward J'avet.

"She didn't. Now she does," he said. Yep, that pretty much summed it up.

Infinity fired back, just a regular old torpedo, but it looked as big as our pod.

Gamma destroyed the torpedo before it even got close and *Infinity* rocked with another blast from the sonic cannon.

"*Gamma's* small, but she takes no shit from anyone," Brinley said.

"Like us," I said with a satisfied smile.

Gamma moved away from *Infinity*, but the bigger ship made no move to follow.

"She's dead in the water," Brinley said. "I would guess she wasn't ready to leave Dendra, but they took her anyway."

"Now we just have to worry about the pod chasing us," I said. I realised without *Infinity*, those on board might become more desperate.

I finished that thought when a loud bang sounded right above my head, and our pod shook. Instinctively, I ducked down, even though the reflex wouldn't save me from anything.

"We're hit," Brinley said.

We began to slow. Where the pod previously vibrated with movement and power, it shuddered and fell still. A moment later, it was filled with smoke.

That didn't seem like a good sign to me.

"They hit a fuel tank," Brinley said. "We can't fly under our own power."

J'avet looked back. "There is a chance the pod may explode. If it does that—"

"We're totally boned," I finished for him. Frankly,

I was getting tired of feeling like I should kiss my ass goodbye.

"Yes," he said softly. "We need to get off this pod."

I cocked my head at him. "That much is obvious. The question is how?" Escape pods didn't generally come with lifeboats.

"When the other pod catches up and clamps on, we'll have to let them board," J'avet said. "That's the only chance we have."

"Well shit," I said under my breath. Looks like we skipped plans A and B and went straight to F. F for fucked up.

9

WE DIDN'T HAVE to wait long. Four or five minutes after we came to a stop, the other pod drew up alongside us.

"Oh look, roadside assist is here," I muttered. Yeah, people still drove cars on Earth, but the joke went over J'avet's head.

Brinley looked too anxious to even smile. "I think it's more like carjacking," she said.

"Right." I grimaced. "We packed blasters, didn't we?"

"Yes, but you won't be using one," J'avet said. "You'll shoot off your own foot. Or mine."

"Hey, I've used blasters before, and we're both still intact." I narrowed my eyes at him. "Actually it was *you* who almost shot off *my* foot."

He looked back at me, face entirely expression-less. He didn't even look slightly apologetic.

I guess we *were* fighting for our lives at the time. Better I lose a foot than my life, although neither was ideal.

"You and Brinley will go to the bunk room, out of the way," he said. "E'rel and I will deal with the Iri."

I wanted to protest. I could kick ass too. Had I not proven that several times already?

On the other hand, I knew that look on his face. He wasn't going to give even half a hair's width.

Forget stubborn as a mule. Stubborn as a Parvoran; they're much worse. I had a feeling E'rel was just as bad.

"Fine," I said reluctantly. Only because the metallic clang of clamps attaching one pod to another echoed and sent chills up and down my spine.

The Iri would be through the door in moments.

I followed Brinley into the bunk room, but we left the door open. Honestly, I wasn't sure it would close, unless it had a manual setting somewhere I didn't know about. Now was not the time to go searching.

The pod's lights blinked and the air got heavier.

I was no engineer, but I had a feeling the Iri hit more than the fuel tank.

"I'm starting to think we weren't supposed to reach Agus," I whispered. It felt like a lifetime since I boarded the shuttle on Earth. I was scared then, but the trip should have been simple and straightforward. A hop to Moon Station, a trip on *Infinity* for a couple of weeks, get off at Agus.

No fuss, no muss. Instead, it was nonstop fuss and a lot of muss.

"We'll get there," Brinley assured me. "Although, by the time we do, we might be the ones doing the teaching. We've done quite a bit of on the job training." Her English accent sounded stronger now, with her anxiety.

I gave her a wry smile. "You're not wrong there, mate." I accentuated my Australian accent.

She smiled in return, then we both ducked down and watched as the pod door started to glow.

E'rel grabbed a device from his box of Slek-tech and tossed it to J'avet. He picked up one of his own and a blaster.

With straight backs, both guys faced the door, blaster in one hand, device in the other.

"What is that?" I asked.

"I'm not sure," Brinley replied. "But they're both hot fully armed like that."

I grinned. As it happens, she was right. Maybe now wasn't the time for those kinds of thoughts, but they came in my head, um, *into* my head, anyway.

The door glowed brighter.

I squinted.

"They couldn't try knocking on the door?" I said softly.

"Some people have no manners," Brinley agreed. "What must their parents think?"

"No idea," I replied. "Kids these days." Okay, the whole conversation was silly, but it helped settle my nerves. I suspected it did the same for Brinley. It certainly didn't hurt. There were worse ways to pass what might be our last few minutes.

A hole appeared in the middle of the door. It quickly expanded until it was big enough to allow an adult to step through.

The smoke was heavier now. Some came from where we were struck, and even more came from whatever they used to melt the door.

At first, I couldn't see through the breach.

I put a hand over my mouth to suppress a cough. The air was thick, but didn't feel quite as heavy now.

The Iri pod must be sharing oxygen with ours. How kind of them.

"Stand down," a voice said from inside the smoke. "Throw down your weapons." The voice sounded unsure and tentative, but almost certainly female.

If I couldn't see, chances were, they couldn't either. If that was the case, they wouldn't know J'avet and E'rel were armed. It was a reasonable guess, but just that: a guess.

"We have no weapons." J'avet must have made the same assumption. "We're on a peaceful mission to take supplies to... Vargo."

I held my breath.

Did the Iri notice his hesitation? What would she make of it if she did? She might assume someone headed for the nearest planet would know its name.

On the other hand, people forget things all the time. Birthdays, anniversaries, planet names. No big deal.

Right?

"This pod is now ours." Apparently it didn't matter if she noticed or not. The Iri wanted the pod, not a friendly conversation.

"I don't think so." The smoke cleared slightly, enough for me to make out J'avet as he stepped forward. His figure wavered, distorted by the thick air. Even though the Iri scared him as much as they scared me, he sounded completely calm. "Actually, your pod is now ours."

I frowned. How did he figure that?

The Iri stepped through the doorway, a blaster in her hand as well.

A shiver passed through me. J'avet could be such an ass, but I didn't want to lose him too.

Hadn't I lost enough already?

No, I reminded myself. The others weren't lost, just…misplaced for a while. We would get through this and I would find them, and then—

I bit back a sob. Brinley's arm went around me and I leaned against her.

"It'll be okay," she whispered. "We'll get through this."

I nodded. My tongue darted over my lips before I said, "Yeah, I hope so."

She gave me a squeeze.

"There's only one of you," J'avet said. "There's two of us."

Now who can't add up? I thought. Of course, he was trying to avoid drawing attention to Brinley and I. I appreciated that. I didn't want to be noticed too much by someone armed and ready to fire.

The Iri cocked her head. The smoke had almost

cleared entirely. The glazed look in her eyes was visible. She was consulting with the nanobot hive mind, or whatever it was.

Finally, she straightened her head. "Our numbers are greater than one. On board the other pod, are others."

J'avet leaned to the side to make a show of looking around her. "I see only you."

"There is only one," E'rel stated. He sounded as robotic as she did. "We should take care of her. We're wasting time." He raised his blaster.

She raised hers just before two more Iri appeared in the doorway.

"Our numbers are more than one," she said again.

"So we see," J'avet said.

"Your numbers are more than two." The Iri turned and aimed her blaster toward the bunk room. She got off a shot that missed my head by a hair. Actually from the smell of singed hair, it didn't miss.

"Fuck." I ducked down further. I almost didn't see J'avet raise the device and point it toward the Iri woman.

She froze.

The Iri behind her took aim at J'avet. Before he fired, E'rel used his device on him. He too froze. J'avet froze the third.

"What the—" Before I finished my question, nanobots started to trickle out of the Iritauri, to lie in a puddle on the pod floor.

I should have known. Part of the box of Slek-tech was a couple of anti-bot devices. He'd managed to switch off the bots on the *Halcyon*, but I hadn't known anyone was working on a personal, handheld version.

Cool.

J'avet exhaled loudly, then moved in a blur to catch the woman before she fell to the floor, face Freytauri blue again. He lowered her down and tried to grab one of the men, but only managed to keep him from falling too hard.

E'rel wasn't close enough to help the last man, who toppled sideways against the door before making a graceful slide to the floor.

None were Danec or Slek, or even Zarex.

"Is that all of them?" I asked as I rose to my feet.

"Stay here." J'avet gestured for E'rel to step through into the other pod with him.

Since he didn't specify where 'here' was, I hurried to crouch beside the former hosts. None seemed to be injured, but they would take time to fully recover from being invaded by nanobots.

I glanced through the doorway. J'avet and E'rel

stood beside another Freytauri, also a woman, device still in their hands.

"There's no one else here," J'avet said. "We'll need to move everything from one pod to another."

E'rel sighed as if he'd been asked to walk the length of a marathon.

I mean, sure, it was a hassle, but at least we were alive.

"We have another problem," Brinley said. "We're not stocked with enough supplies or fuel for eight." She'd already made herself comfortable in the pilot's seat of the new pod and checked over the controls. At least, I think that was what she was doing.

"We'll need to take them to the *Gamma*," J'avet said. He looked as impressed as E'rel, but this time with good reason. Taking the former hosts to the ship would take time and delay our mission. Still, it couldn't be helped. *Gamma* was a better place for them than here.

"At least we know those anti-bot things work," I said. Even when he wasn't here, Slek was helping us. "Have we got any more of them?"

E'rel looked at me as if he thought I was the last person on board who should have one.

"Three more," he said finally. "I'm working on a fourth. We need many more."

J'avet nodded. "The sooner you get back to work, the sooner we will have them." To Brinley, he said, "Plot a course to meet up with *Gamma* and let Captain Marshall know we're coming."

Brinley nodded. "Done and done. There's four, no five, IF ships approaching. They seem to be heading toward *Infinity*."

"That will keep them busy." J'avet looked satisfied at that. "I'll send them the specifications for Slek's ship-wide...anti-bot device." He gave me the faintest of smiles to acknowledge his adoption of my term. It was as good a one as any.

I shrugged and turned to help the first Freytauri woman to sit up.

"What happened?" She looked dazed and confused.

I couldn't blame her. We had probably come close to dying only several minutes earlier, and she held the blaster. None of that was her fault, but she might not see it that way. It didn't matter what species someone was, people always seemed ready to blame themselves for all sorts of things.

"Nanobots happened," I said. "You're free of them and their influence." I needed her to know there were no hard feelings for anything the bots made her do. None of it was her.

"They're switched off." For now. "We're headed to another ship. They'll take you to wherever you need to go." I offered her a smile.

She replied with a confused frown. "Um. Okay, I guess." She looked around, obviously with no idea how she got there.

From what I'd seen of Iri nanobot infestation, she would remember everything in time. When she did, she'd need a lot of support to deal with it. I didn't envy her, or any of them.

I patted her shoulder. "Come on, we need to get into the other pod. This one isn't safe."

With my help, she stood and tottered on unsteady legs until she could flop down onto a bunk.

The other three managed by themselves, but the effort to move under their own power was obviously great. The strain on their faces spoke volumes.

I left them there to rest, then helped J'avet carry the food and fuel from one pod to the other. Even E'rel helped, once his corner was all moved over.

The old pod cleared of anything but inactive nanobots, J'avet closed the door.

"Disengage the clamps and move us a safe distance away," he said.

"Declamping and getting clear," Brinley confirmed.

We drew closer to *Gamma*, which was stationary until J'avet opened the comms.

"*Gamma*. Anytime you want to laser that pod, we're clear."

Marshall's voice came back. "Commander, I thought you'd never ask." She sounded as though she couldn't imagine anything more fun.

A weapons port on the side of the ship opened. Something inside it moved, like the muzzle of a canon turning to lock onto a target. A flash of laser shot out, so brilliant it lit up the galaxy. At least, our little bit of it.

I squinted against the glare.

The laser slammed into the pod. For a moment, nothing happened. Then the pod exploded, blowing it and all the nanobots into oblivion.

"You're cleared to dock," Marshall declared, satisfaction in her tone. "All aboard."

10

"WELCOME TO THE *GAMMA*." The captain and two security officers greeted J'avet and I as we stepped off the pod.

Brinley and E'rel stayed back to gather E'rel's devices. The Parvoran was adamant they not be left behind for a moment, and J'avet agreed. Honestly, so did I. Trust was a hard commodity to find lately, what with all the nanobots running around the galaxy.

"Thank you, Captain," J'avet said, his tone and expression distracted.

"You're welcome, Commander." Captain Marshall eyed him as though amused by something. She was taller than me, and more slender. The hair at her temples was grey. Lines on her face suggested she smiled a lot.

I suspected she didn't miss anything, ever. I bet nothing happened on her ship that she wasn't aware of. I would bet just about anything she took even less shit than I did. That was saying something.

She reminded me of Doctor Kalvix, who died on *Infinity*. That in turn made me think of how Slek had flirted with the doctor. He would flirt with the captain too, I suspected. Hopefully, I would find that out for sure soon.

It couldn't come soon enough.

"Thank you, Captain," J'avet said again. "We'll be on our way as soon as the Freytauri are transferred to the infirmary."

In spite of his firm tone, Marshall smiled. The kind of smile that said he wouldn't like what she was about to say, but that was too bad. "You'll be here a while longer than that. Admiral's orders."

J'avet scowled. "You said we were to be allowed to go on our way. I appreciate the need for *Gamma* to follow at a discreet distance, but—"

"Things change," Marshall said shortly. "You've proven that one small pod is too vulnerable." Her eyes were like pools of steel, hard and uncompromising.

Still, I had to try. "We dealt with the Iritauri," I pointed out. "We just don't have room for more on the pod. We'd run out of oxygen and fuel before we reached Iritauri space." There was no point in freeing the hosts only to have them suffocate along with us a couple of days later. Besides, I didn't want to share the cans of frankfurts with anyone else.

J'avet gave a sharp nod. "We have a greater chance of success—"

Marshall held up her hands to cut him off. "Argue with the admiral. I'm simply following orders. You will all remain on board *Gamma* until we get closer to Iri space."

"Then what?" I asked. I had the funny feeling they wouldn't simply let us go again, now we were here. Was there room in the brig for four of us?

"Then we await further orders," Marshall said evenly. She lowered her hands as though the conversation was finished.

Evidently it wasn't as far as J'avet was concerned. "Since when did you follow blindly?" he asked, his voice almost a growl.

The side of her mouth twitched in annoyance. "Since the future of the entire galaxy was at stake," she replied. "I know this is hard to believe, but this is bigger than you, Commander."

I choked back an ironic laugh. I'd lost track of the amount of times I assumed J'avet thought himself more important than whatever went on around him. This time though, I *knew* he knew otherwise. He was doing all of this for the good of everyone.

J'avet gave her a cold stare. "I know that, Captain," he said through gritted teeth. "That's why I don't want this mission fucked up by someone behind a desk."

"He has a good point," I said before Marshall had a chance to respond angrily. "J'avet knows where to go. We need to get in there undetected. Someone who has never even met an Iri, much less dealt with one—"

"Is still in charge," Marshall said firmly.

If I didn't think it would get me into trouble, I might have pointed out how rude it was to interrupt. She'd done it three times since we stepped off the pod.

"We've set aside cabins for you all," Marshall went on as though we hadn't spoken at all. "Take what you need from the pod, you'll be locked out of the pod bay. Just in case."

J'avet's eyes flashed. If he could shoot lasers out of them, I'm sure he would have.

We couldn't even argue this point, really. We *had*

tried to steal a pod in the first place. Just because we'd been allowed to didn't mean we were off the hook for that.

"Yes, Captain," he said finally. He'd already grabbed his bag. Apparently that was all he needed because he headed toward the pod bay doors without even a glance back at me.

"He's such a charmer," Marshall said dryly.

"He's okay," I said. "Kind of." He had his moments. If he thought I would trot after him, he would have to think again.

"I'll help the others." I stepped aside to let a couple of security officers and the four Freytauri step off the pod. The former hosts still looked dazed, but judging by the haunted looks in their eyes, their memories were returning. I didn't envy them for a moment. The anguish they would suffer for the next while would be immense. Likely, they would never fully recover.

Before they could take more than a couple of steps away from the pod, I stopped them to ask, "I don't suppose you know a Danec, son of Jaek, or Slek, son of Arron, do you?"

They all gave me the same blank look and faint head shake, before the security officers urged them to trudge on.

"Friends of yours?" Marshall asked. She seemed genuinely interested.

"Yeah," I said, but my guard was up. I decided against telling her more, in case she decided I was too close, emotionally, to handle the mission. Unlike J'avet, I didn't work for GASP, so technically I didn't answer to Marshall.

On the other hand, I was pretty sure if she wanted me out of the way, she would do it, and apologise to the medical arm of the IF later. Or not apologise. I didn't think she'd actually be sorry for anything she did. She didn't get to captain a ship without being confident with her choices.

"Go and help your teammates." She nodded toward the pod. "Then get some rest. You look like you need it. And make sure J'avet sees a doctor, or I will." She turned and walked away.

"I'm not his keeper," I said under my breath and to her back. I headed back into the pod.

"I don't suppose there's any chance of sneaking back off *Gamma?*" I asked.

Brinley glanced up from the bag she was placing tools into. "Probably not, no. Why?"

I told her what Marshall said. By the time I finished, Brinley was frowning. E'rel wore his customary scowl.

"I guess we're safer on here anyway," I said, as if I didn't feel defeated.

"Do you think she'll let us off when we reach Iri space?" Brinley asked. "She might be imagining the glory of defeating those nanobots." She grimaced.

"If we don't proceed with stealth, we will fail," E'rel said bluntly. "Her ego may doom the galaxy."

That would make a great tagline for a book or movie, but in real life it scared the shit out of me.

"We'll have to do whatever we can to make sure that doesn't happen," I said firmly. "This is bigger than her, too."

I turned my face slightly to see a security officer standing near the doorway. No doubt he'd heard everything we said. We'd have to watch ourselves. Although, we hadn't said anything we wouldn't want Marshall to hear.

Yet.

"Here." I reached for one of the bags and swung it over my shoulder along with my own bag. "Lucky we didn't unpack when we left the other pod."

Brinley smiled. "Yeah. We didn't even have time to get comfortable."

"No one could get comfortable on a pod," E'rel grumbled.

"Oh, I don't know," I said lightly. "It's better than a

tent. Unless you're being fired on."

"I'd rather be fired on in a pod than in a tent," Brinley said. "The chance of surviving is slightly higher."

"Approximately 52 percent higher," E'rel said. "You cannot flee from a pod which is in space." He frowned as if annoyed at himself for taking part in our silly conversation.

"Good point," I said cheerfully. "At least we can flee from this one." I stepped back out of the pod and flashed the Agusian security officer a warm smile.

He gave me a funny look and his antennas bent to follow me as I moved away. For someone of the same species, he didn't look much like Zarex, but the antenna action made me miss the commander acutely.

I wanted to fast forward to when this was over and we were all safe. If only life worked that way.

We stepped out the pod bay doors, only to be greeted by yet more security officers.

"We'll show you to your cabins," one said.

I had a sense of déjà vu. After the attack on *Infinity*, we were 'guests' on board another ship.

Way too many bad things were becoming a habit lately.

"You could just give us the numbers," I said. "We

can find it ourselves."

"Captain's orders. She doesn't want to risk you getting lost."

"This ship isn't big enough to get lost," E'rel said. Clearly he was as tired of their bullshit as I was.

The security officer shrugged. "I'm just following orders. I'm sure you understand."

"We do," Brinley said, her tone nicer than I could have managed. "Lead on, please." She sounded like she was asking to be taken to a nice tea room, one that served scones with whipped cream.

Great, now I was hungry.

The Agusian gestured for us to follow him. A Dendran officer fell in behind us.

"I'm having a flashback to Calig," I remarked."Only these guys don't have bows and arrows."

"And they're not going to kill us, or infest us with nanobots," Brinley said firmly.

"I hope not," I replied. I eyed the Agusian. He didn't seem offended by this line of conversation.

Personally, I would be annoyed if someone compared me to people the nanobots reduced to little more than mindless, murder puppets.

"You're perfectly safe on board *Gamma*," the Dendran assured us.

"Until someone fires on us all," I said.

She hesitated. "Until then, yes. *Gamma* is more than equipped to take care of herself, as you no doubt saw."

I nodded. "I saw." That gave me some comfort. She'd stood up to *Infinity* better than we would have on our own. "They are freeing all those on *Infinity* from the nanobots, aren't they?" I asked.

"I don't have any information on that," she said.

She reminded me of the automated voice I had on an old so-called smart watch. Good for setting timers and doing maths my lazy ass didn't want to bother with, but more often than not, it had no useful answers.

"Right. Well, when you know, can you let us know, please?" I couldn't rule out the possibility the guys were on that ship. I would have liked to board *Infinity* to check, but it was unlikely I'd be allowed to. If I was, I probably wouldn't be allowed back on *Gamma*.

All I could do was hope that if they were on there, they would contact me the first chance they got.

"If I can, I will," she said.

I guessed that was about the best I would get.

The officers led us to the back of the ship and

waved toward a set of doors.

"You'll have to share. *Gamma* isn't equipped for guests," the Agusian said.

The doors slid apart without a sound.

J'avet stood with his back to us, looking out to space. He didn't turn until the doors closed behind us and we started to place our bags on the narrow bunks.

"Can you believe this?" I asked.

He grunted.

"Yeah, I agree," I said, as though I understood grunt-ese. "It's a total pain in the ass."

He regarded me through narrowed eyes. "You really never shut up, do you?"

"Nope," I said lightly. "Hey look, a shower. I could use a wash."

"I could use some food," Brinley said. She gripped E'rel's hand and pulled him toward the door. "Come on, let's eat."

He looked pained, but left anyway.

"Do you need to eat?" I asked J'avet.

He shook his head. "No." He looked hungry, but not for food. "Come here."

I looked at him sideways, but stepped forward. The moment I was close enough, he tangled his hand in my hair and pushed me to my knees.

"I know one way to shut you up," he growled. With his spare hand, he undid his pants and pushed down the front. His public plate slid aside to reveal his already erect cock. He dragged me forward until he was able to shove his cock into my mouth.

Yep, he was right. I couldn't talk like this.

I ran the tip of my tongue over his cock and tasted his juices.

He groaned and pushed his cock in deeper.

"Suck," he ordered.

Normally I don't like being ordered around, but since I was already there, I might as well.

I sucked gently, while my hand crept up to search his groin. I wasn't sure what I would find there, but my fingers touched balls that felt like those of any other guy I had been with.

He moaned. "Harder." His hips moved back and forth as he fucked my mouth deeper and deeper.

I sucked harder at the same time as I cupped his balls and toyed with them.

I thought he was about to come when he pulled out of me.

"Shower," he said. Apparently the blood abandoned his brain to the point he could only say one word at a time.

He pulled me to my feet and all but tore my

clothes off before we were both immersed in hot water. He pressed me against the wall and hooked one of my legs around his hip.

Without another word, he slid three fingers inside me and started to rub me with firm, hard strokes.

In approximately three point two seconds, I was ready to come. I guess I needed this more than I knew.

I panted out a moan and threw back my head, narrowly missing the wall before I stopped. Knocking myself unconscious would be a really crappy thing to do in the middle of sex.

J'avet stroked me harder still, so hard he grunted with the effort.

My hips bucked frantically several times before I came. A fierce growl of pleasure slipped out from between my lips. If anything squirted from my other lips, it was washed away in the water.

I hadn't even started to come down when he drew his hand out of me, bent me so my face was under the flow of water, and slammed his cock into me from behind.

The water was too hot and the pressure so strong, I had to move my head to the side every so often just to get a breath.

His hand, which had left my hair while we undressed, wound into my curls again.

He held me firm under the water while he pounded again and again with no hint of restraint.

My head felt light. I was forced to pull him, hand and all, to the side so I could breathe.

He didn't go easily. I thought he might tear out a handful of hair. The pain was both terrible and exquisite. If he was anyone else, I might have told him to stop. I knew he would if I asked.

That was exactly why I didn't. I let him dominate me, and that permission, which I could revoke at any time, gave me the power. I had as much say in all of this as he did. If I didn't want him to hammer my entrance, he wouldn't. If I hadn't wanted a throatful of his cock, I wouldn't have had one. I knew he knew all of this, even though he hadn't hesitated for a moment.

"Fuck...Edie," he ground out.

That was the idea here. I might have laughed, but I'd end up with a mouthful of water. That, I didn't want.

He slammed a few more times, then pulled out of me. He turned me around and put his hands under my arms. With almost no effort, he lifted me until I could wrap my legs around him. He guided his cock back into me and thrust again, more sedately this time.

With one hand, he held me in place, while the other explored my breasts and pinched my nipples.

"You are..." he said slowly, each word an obvious effort, "mine. Even when we get the others back. Choose us all if you have to. I'm not giving you up."

He ground his groin against me and pressed me against the shower wall.

The only response I could manage was, "Okay." That was a bridge we could cross when we reached it, but I couldn't imagine not having them all in my life.

He thrust slower, then faster, but always with as much force as he could put behind it. He wasn't a man who did things by halves. Whatever he did, he shoved every bit of himself into it. I wasn't sure if that meant he enjoyed life, or was trying to throttle the hells out of it.

Either way, he made for a fun fuck.

I closed my eyes and let the sensation of desire grow again. His cock hit me deep inside, in just the right place. Again and again he hit, as though he could force an orgasm out of me. Maybe he could, because I came again, more intense this time and lasting longer. Unlike the first, this time he milked it for every bit of sensation he could get into me.

Then he came with a guttural grunt that sounded so primal, I wondered if he was a wild animal, at least for a moment.

He ground into me for what felt like a lifetime, then sagged forward, out of breath. He wound his arms around me and drew me to him, holding me in spite of how slippery I must be by now.

His cock worked free as I placed my head on his damp shoulder.

My eyes flickered shut and I rested all of my weight on him.

"There, that shut me up," I whispered.

He snorted near my ear. "For a while. I might have to keep you quiet for longer yet."

"Oh yeah? How will you do that?" I asked.

He nibbled at the side of my neck, grazing his teeth over my skin.

"I'll find a way," he assured me. He lowered me down and grabbed up a bar of soap. "But first, we wash." He turned me around and started to run soap up and down my body.

I sighed and let him work his magic while the hot water soothed my muscles.

11

I WOKE up squashed against the wall, J'avet fast asleep beside me.

I checked my watch. It was almost five am. The whole ship would awaken soon. Part of me wished time would hurry. The other part wished it would stop completely. I wasn't particularly comfortable, but I could sleep for a month. Better yet, sleep surrounded by all the guys.

The bed shifted and I found myself with room to roll over. I couldn't manage to fully open my eyes yet. Like every other ship, I'd worked in the infirmary during our time on board. Like every infirmary, there were never enough hours or staff. Even for a relatively small ship, something always needed to be done. In particular, the former hosts needed a lot of care. I'd spent hours talking to them, letting them share the trauma they'd been through.

At least, what they were ready to deal with.

One of the women, an engineer named Kariz, had worked on the repairs to *Infinity*. She told me how everything was going well enough, until power shut down, seemingly at random. She hadn't seen the nanobots before they flooded into her system, but she and other now Iri engineers turned the systems back on and took the ship out of dry dock.

The next thing she knew, *Infinity* attacked *Gamma* and the bots in her head made her step onto the pod and attack us.

Then she was back to herself again, and grateful for it.

"I knew what was going on the whole time," she told me. "But I couldn't stop it. I couldn't stop *myself*. I wanted to send out a distress beacon, or destroy *Infinity*, but I couldn't."

She cried on my shoulder while I patted her back and said words I hoped would soothe her. Honestly, I wasn't sure I helped much. Only time and therapy would do that.

How hard would it be for Danec to come back after weeks, months as a host? The thought of him struggling to come to terms with everything threatened to break my heart. He would have all the support he could manage, and then some, but the sooner we got him back, the better.

"Edie. Time to get up." J'avet's voice broke through my sleepy musing.

I groaned and rolled over to face the wall.

"Or I can leave you out of this meeting," he said. "You shouldn't be there anyway."

I sat up so fast I hit my head on the bunk above.

"Ouch." I rubbed my head. "I'm going."

"Then you need to get up," he said again. "We won't wait for you."

I cracked open my eyes. He was already dressed except for a couple of buttons he was doing up now.

Brinley and E'rel were nowhere to be seen.

"They've gone to breakfast," J'avet said.

"Are you reading my mind now?" I pushed off the blanket and stood, aware of J'avet's eyes on my naked body. Once, I would have hidden from anyone's gaze. Now, I felt pretty, knowing he looked admiringly and not in a judgemental way.

"I wouldn't," he replied. "I'm sure it's as messy in there as your hair is."

Okay, he was a bit judgy.

I stuck out my tongue at him and started to put on my clothes. Jeans and a cute blue t-shirt that would have looked better on Brinley than me. Whatever, it was comfortable, and more or less said 'I'm not on nurse duty today.' It wouldn't stop me from working if I was needed, of course, but it felt nice to be casual.

"For your information, my mind is an organised place," I said as I sat on the floor to pull on some socks. "Everything is neatly filed away, like a database." Or like a wiki, where people added and deleted stuff at random, so you never quite knew what was real and what wasn't. I didn't know how half the stuff in my brain got in there.

Also, I had a special file for 'weird alien dicks,' but doesn't every girl? If not, then she should. The ones I'd met were worthy of their own file each.

"Are you nearly ready?" J'avet tossed me my hairbrush while I stood.

I managed to catch it and drag it through my crazy curls. I could use a trim. Sometimes I envied the guys their short, military haircuts. I could do that too, but I doubted I would rock the look. I wasn't sure I rocked this look either, but it was the only look I had.

Half way through brushing, I caught J'avet staring at me, a slight frown on his face.

"What?" I asked. "Do I have cum on my face?"

He looked surprised, then actually smiled. "No. I was thinking how strange it is that humans have so much hair on their heads and so little on their bodies."

Hmmm, what do you know, I wasn't the only one thinking about weird alien attributes.

I shrugged. "And I'm pink." If I was covered in the same light hair he was, I might be brown, like a bear. As cute as that sounded, I think I'll stick to peach-coloured.

"More pink in some places than others," he said, looking toward my breasts.

I blushed then and tried to focus on untangling the last of my curls.

"If I didn't know better," I said, brushing furiously, "I would think you're flirting with me."

"Parvorans don't flirt," he scoffed. "We state what we want to say. Your nipples are pink. And you'll be late if you don't hurry." He turned toward the door.

"Parvorans could use some manners," I said. "The polite thing to do would be to wait a moment until I'm ready."

He turned back, his frown deeper. "What would that achieve? We would both be late."

"Yes, but we'd arrive together," I said.

"I see no benefit in us *both* arriving late." He seemed genuinely confused.

"It's not about us arriving late, it's about you being a gentleman and waiting." I tossed the brush on the bed and crossed my arms.

"Gentle man," he said slowly. "I can be gentle, but you seemed to like it—"

I shook my head. "That's not—" I exhaled in frustration. "It doesn't matter, I'm ready now anyway. Let's go."

With obvious relief on his face, he opened the door. When they said men and women were from different planets, they hadn't meant it literally, but they might as well have. Since we actually did, it made the differences between us greater and more confusing.

I put it out of my mind and followed him down the corridor to the small meeting room. Brinley and E'rel were already there. The moment I stepped inside, Brinley handed me coffee and a slice of toast.

"You are my hero," I told her.

E'rel and J'avet exchanged glances.

"Humans like it when you bring them food," J'avet explained.

"Ah." E'rel flopped into a chair with no indication he was moved by the valuable piece of information he'd been given. He now had the key to moving past fights with Brinley, but he didn't seem to realise it.

"Especially chocolate," I said around a mouthful of toast. "And coffee or tea."

"Or alcohol," Brinley said.

"Or that," I agreed. "It all helps."

"But not too much food," J'avet said. "Human women are often watching their weight."

"Yes we are, but you never, ever get to comment on it." I narrowed my eyes at J'avet. He had done that once and was lucky I hadn't grabbed a stick and poked him in the eye for it.

"You humans are strange," E'rel said.

"That we are," Marshall said as she stepped into the room. "But we make up for it by being awesome. Now, we're approaching Iritauri space."

The sudden change in subject almost gave me whiplash. I slipped into a chair and sipped my coffee.

"I've spoken to the admiral about whether or not you'll be allowed to proceed in the pod." Marshall leaned against the doorway and regarded us all in a way that suggested she held all the cards and she knew it.

"What was the admiral's conclusion?" J'avet said, effectively reminding us all that the admiral held the whole pack. Marshall was a subordinate, just like the rest of us.

If the reminder annoyed her, she gave no sign outside the twitch of one side of her mouth.

"In spite of my better judgement, the admiral is letting you go," Marshall said. "However, *Gamma* will remain at a discreet distance behind the pod and engage any enemies. The mission remains the same. Stealth. During your time on board, Engineer E'rel has worked with my team to produce more devices such as the one which freed our four former-host guests. My chief engineer reports that she'd like more time to work on them, but we no longer have the luxury of time. We will move forward with what we have."

She rolled her shoulders for a moment. "Because the time on board *Gamma* has minimised the pod's fuel use, I'm able to assign four security officers to accompany you. They will operate under the orders of Commander J'avet." She eyed him. "Don't get them killed."

J'avet's mouth was set in a line. "My intention is never to get anyone killed."

"Yeah. Shit happens," Marshall said. "With four more trained, armed personnel, maybe we can minimise the shit and get the job done."

She turned her eyes on me and I had the idea she was about to say something I didn't like.

"I don't feel comfortable sending a civilian into what might end up as a conflict situation."

"I'd be lying if I said I felt comfortable going," I said. "But I'm still going. I've dealt with Iri before. And former Iri." I lifted my chin. I would stow away if I had to, but I wasn't being left out. My guys were out there and I wouldn't rest until I got them back.

"That's why the admiral is letting you go," Marshall said. "I suggested you would find a way to get back on board that pod."

"Damn right I would," I said. "When do we leave?"

"Within the hour," Marshall replied. "The engineers are finishing up some modifications to the pod, and making sure it's fully stocked with everything you need. Engineer E'rel, I'm sure you'll want to oversee the work." She jerked her head toward the door.

"Yes, I would." He hurried out without a backward glance.

Maybe Parvorans weren't assholes, they just hadn't learnt any manners. I've never been the kind of girl who tries to change a guy, so I guess I would have to get used to it. Who knows, they might pick up a thing or two in time.

"Pilot Brinley, you'll see the controls are now equipped with a tracker. We want to know the pod's whereabouts at all times." Marshall fixed her gaze on Brinley, who nodded.

"However," Marshall continued, "the tracker goes both ways, and has longer reach than the pod's existing sensors. You'll know the location of *Gamma* at all times, as well as any other ships, IF or otherwise, even at a few hundred kilometres distance. You can also shout for help and be heard sooner."

I sat back in my chair and asked, "If we ask for help, will any ship hear it?"

Marshall looked at me as though I asked a really good question. "Yes," she replied. "If you only want to speak to *Gamma*, you'll need to use the pod's usual comms. If you use the tracker, the Iri will hear it, too. We don't have time to modify it further."

"It will do," J'avet said.

"It will have to." Marshall straightened up. "We've done what we could while you were our visitors, but after this, you're on your own. I wish you luck on this mission. I'm sure you know how important it is."

"The future of the galaxy rests on our success," J'avet said.

No pressure.

My heart raced and my palms sweated like crazy.

This was so much more than a rescue mission to save the guys. If we failed, the galaxy might well be fucked. Overrun by nanobots bent on domination.

Yep, we only had one option here, as I saw it. Don't fail. Absolutely no pressure at all, no way.

Shit.

12

THE SECURITY OFFICERS were waiting when we reached the pod. Three were Agusian and the fourth was a Garvian.

One Agusian, a tall guy who reminded me a lot of Zarex, stepped forward.

"I am Rayax. This is Tarvun and Navor." He gestured toward the other two Agusians. "And Hamit."

The Garvian nodded. The movement made his tentacles flip and flop.

Another time, I might have laughed, but my sense of humour seemed to have taken a hike somewhere. Maybe it was the collection of long faces around me. Everyone looked anxious, but determined.

"Edie, Brinley, J'avet," J'avet said. "E'rel should be inside the pod. We all should."

If Rayax was bothered by J'avet's brusque tone, he didn't show it. He simply saluted and waved for us to precede him inside.

J'avet barely acknowledged him, just walked past and into the pod, followed by Brinley.

I gave Rayax a shrug and he responded with a wink. Yep, he reminded me even more of Zarex. Before I could say a word, he spoke softly, "Zarex is my brother. I managed to work it so I could come too. I want him back as much as anyone."

Once I got past my surprise, I smiled and patted his arm. "We'll find him," I promised. "He's probably given them so much trouble by now, they'll be glad to hand him back to us." Hopefully not so much trouble they killed him. No, I wouldn't think about that. I couldn't. Just the idea hurt my heart too much.

Rayan responded with a wry smile. "That sounds like him." His expression faded into one of concern that mirrored my feelings exactly. Zarex has that effect on people, obviously. He's easy to care about.

Rayax stepped away so I could board.

"He's cute," Brinley said as I swung my bag onto an empty bunk.

"You don't think I have my hands full enough?" I asked.

She smiled. "Knowing you, you'd handle one more. Or several." Other women might be jealous, but she was happy for me.

"Maybe you should continue your own collection," I suggested. "That would keep E'rel on his toes."

She glanced speculatively toward Rayax. "Maybe I will," she said thoughtfully. "In the meantime, I better get this pod underway before the captain changes her mind about letting us go."

"I think at this point, if she does that, J'avet will tell you to fly through the pod bay doors." I knew full well that would only result in the destruction of the pod, but I was done being told we can't do this or that. I just wanted to be on our way.

Brinley smiled and hurried to the cockpit, where J'avet already sat. He seemed to be looking over the controls, possibly trying to locate the tracker.

I leaned down so my mouth was near his ear.

"Are you going to disable it?" I asked.

"Why would I do that?" he asked over his shoulder.

"Because if *Gamma* can track us, who else can?" I asked.

He twisted around and gaped at me. Without responding, he jumped up and stalked toward E'rel. He crouched beside the other Parvoran and they spoke in low, sharp tones. Whatever they were saying, J'avet wasn't happy.

After a minute or two, he rose and stalked back to the cockpit. He slipped back into a seat and sat with a straight back. "E'rel doesn't know, but he said it's possible for the Iri to pick up our signal if they know to look."

"They're Iritauri," I said, "they'll *know* to look."

"Yes," J'avet said simply. "There's nothing we can do right now. Let's get off this ship. Find a seat and get strapped in."

"Right." I moved to the passenger section and sat in the first row. I felt a bit like the goodie-goodie at school, but I was as close to J'avet and Brinley as I could be without sitting on their laps. As tempting as it might be to sit on J'avet's, it wasn't safe. Especially if we actually had to punch our way out the door.

"What makes a human hunt Iri hosts?" Tarvun sat down beside me and clicked his harness into place.

"Same as you, I would think," I said. "The desire to free all those Freytaurians from their evil clutches."

"Do you really think they are evil?" he asked.

I paused. "The hosts themselves?" I asked slowly. "No. Whoever is behind them, yes. I mean, you'd have to be evil to plot galactic domination, wouldn't you?"

"I suppose you would," he agreed. "Unless you thought the galaxy was better off as hosts."

"Do you?" I asked. This was a strange conversation, for sure.

"Certainly not," he replied. "Freedom is something all species should have."

"Tarvun fancies himself as a philosopher." Rayax sat behind Tarvun and gave him a fond smile.

"He thinks too much." Navor took a seat beside Rayax.

"Maybe you don't think enough," Tarvun suggested.

Navor scratched his antenna. "It doesn't pay to think too much," he said. "Thinking is overrated."

"How would you know?" Tarvun asked, clearly teasing.

"I've seen you do it for the last year and it hasn't made you happy yet," Navor said.

"Excuse them." Hamit sat on the other side of me. "They're always like this. Captain Marshall should probably break them up, but she hasn't done it yet.

Probably because they would complain and drive her to distraction."

"Navor would complain," Tarvun said. "He would miss me too much."

"Says you," Navor said.

I couldn't help but smile at them, especially the glances between Rayax and Tarvun. They obviously had something going on. I couldn't complain about anyone else mixing business with pleasure. I suspected if Brinley started anything with Rayax, Tarvun would come too, as part of the deal. Who ever said we led simple lives? Our love lives were as messy as my hair, as J'avet would say.

The pod engines thrummed and we lifted off the deck.

"Navor might need to know where the vomit bags are," Tarvun remarked.

When I looked at them in alarm, they all grinned.

"Don't scare the poor girl like that," Hamit scolded. "It was only one time he was sick while on a pod."

"Yes," Navor agreed. "I ate too many of those things you humans love. Tacos?"

"Oh." I smiled. "Yeah, they are addictive, aren't they? I mean, not literally." Although…

"Those and nachos. Humans know how to make food," Navor said appreciatively.

"I'm glad we're able to make some kind of contribution to the galaxy," I said. No, really, I was worried all we'd ever bring to the IF were pink nipples and drinking beer out of a shoe. Both of those are amazing, obviously, but nothing in comparison to space travel and the show *Centauri Shores*. Yeah, TV shows are still trashy, but they all go well with popcorn and a few glasses of alcohol.

"I'm sure humans have done a lot to advance the IF," Rayax said. "Like…"

I waited.

He looked apologetic and shrugged. "Humans are cute?" he finally offered.

"No argument from me," I said. What else could I say? He wasn't wrong there.

I looked toward the cockpit window to see we'd already left the pod bay and were almost clear of *Gamma*. A few moments later, we slipped smoothly out into space.

"Set the course," J'avet said.

"Setting course out of IF space," Brinley confirmed.

I could tell by the set of their backs, they were both anticipating something more than just leaving

Gamma behind us. Were they waiting for a chance to disengage the tracker? We might be safer without it, but we'd also be that much more alone out here.

In spite of stealth being the idea, I would have loved to have an army behind me. Or in front of me. Around me would work too; I wasn't fussy. Without some sort of help, we might disappear into the dark, never to be seen again. That would suck.

"So, tell us about these Iri," Rayax said. "From what I gather, they can only assimilate Freytauri. What would they want with my brother?"

His companions obviously knew the details, because none looked surprised.

I told them what I knew, from the first meeting with the Iri on Calig, to the last on *Halcyon*.

"They're trying to alter their programming so they can use all the species as hosts, not just Freytauri," I said finally. "Which is one reason we're trying to deal with them quickly. If we're lucky, we can get to them before they crack the puzzle. If not, we're boned."

Hamit blinked at me a couple of times. "Boned?"

"Yeah. Fucked. Screwed." Danec was right, we did have a lot of words for sex. "In big, big trouble."

"Oh." Hamit got that at last. "How interesting your language is. We would indeed be... boned."

"Let's make sure that doesn't happen," Rayax said firmly.

"Sounds good to me." In the corner of my eye, I watched E'rel move toward the cockpit. I think he believed he was being subtle, but he moved like he had a big sign over his head saying 'I'm up to something.'

Five pairs of eyes followed him. He sat in the seat beside J'avet and pressed a bunch of buttons.

Apparently unable to contain his suspicion, Rayax undid his harness and stood. "I don't think you should touch—"

"Commander J'avet." Marshall's voice came over the comms. "Are you aware the tracker is no longer transmitting?"

"It seems to have failed," J'avet said unapologetically. "I'll have my engineer look into it. I'm sure he'll have it fixed in no time."

E'rel pulled a device off the side of the controls and held it in his palm. "I'll do my best," he said, his expression deadpan.

Brinley's face was pink with the effort not to laugh.

I had no such problem. The tracker might get us killed. That was a good reason to crack open a window and throw it out. Figuratively, of course, because doing that literally would kill us all.

"You said it yourself, we needed more time to get the tracker working correctly," J'avet said. "We'll have to take that time now."

Marshall didn't sound convinced when she replied with, "All right. Keep me informed."

"Yes, Captain." J'avet killed the comms connection. "Toss that thing in a box and leave it there. We have more important things to work on."

E'rel nodded and returned to his corner, muttering something about wastes of good materials, under his breath.

"Care to explain?" Rayax asked J'avet.

"Not really," J'avet replied. "Apart from the tracker being a danger to us. Are you really here to help?"

Rayax bristled. "Zarex is my brother, he—"

J'avet rolled his eyes. "That explains it."

"J'avet and Zarex have a clash of personalities," I explained.

"Zarex can be…" Rayax searched for the words.

"Yes, he can," J'avet said. "If you're here to help us, then can you explain why anyone would install a device on this pod which might lead the Iritauri directly to us?"

Rayax rolled back onto his heels. "I have no idea. Perhaps it was done in error? Or simply wasn't thought through."

"If you're trying to save the galaxy from a grave threat, then you think *everything* through, right to the end," J'avet said coldly. "To. The. End."

Rayax slumped against the wall. "You're right."

"What can you tell us about the engineer on *Gamma?*" I asked. "They didn't have silver skin, did they?"

"No. She's human, like the captain," Rayax said.

"I hate to say this," I said slowly, "but I don't suppose it's possible someone wants everyone to become hosts, knowing humans can't?" It wouldn't be the first time humans tried to take advantage of a situation so they could take over a country, a city, whatever.

"There's no guarantee humans can't," J'avet said. "Whatever is going on, we'll have to watch our backs. Literally and figuratively." J'avet gave us all a look like he couldn't trust any of us.

After the last few days, that stung. I would have told him to fuck off if we were alone.

"In the meantime, E'rel can analyse the tracker and see if it's programmed to send information to anyone in particular." J'avet turned away and I slouched in my seat.

I wanted to trust all of them, but right now I wasn't sure if I could trust myself. That was the worst part of all. I was on a pod full of people I liked, but I never felt so alone.

13

"We're passing out of IF space," Brinley declared a day or so after we left *Gamma*. "No sign of Iri ships. Or anyone else in front of us. *Gamma* is still on course behind us."

"This has gone very smoothly so far," Rayax remarked.

"I'm as worried about that as you are," I said. I expected to be attacked hours ago, or at least see signs of Iri activity. Ships, pods, debris, floating clouds of nanobots—something.

"The fact nothing has happened may be an indication of something happening," Hamit said.

When I looked at him questioningly, he explained, "They may be avoiding us. Or letting us go in deeper before they act."

"You think they know we're here?" I asked. That wasn't a cheery thought. Not at all. It made me damp under the armpits.

"Possibly," he replied. "Possibly not. Those are merely two theories ."

"Hamit is the most popular member of the team for a reason," Tarvun said. "He's always so positive."

"I'm being realistic," Hamit retorted. "There's no point in pretending we're on a journey to find a pleasant place to eat our midday meal."

"Right, this is no picnic," I agreed. "For one thing, there are no tacos. Are there tacos on Agus?"

"They were one of the first Earth foods to be imported there, yes," Rayax said. He sounded jovial, but his antennas drooped slightly. The worry in his eyes added to the picture. He looked at me and smiled, his antennas suddenly fully erect, but I already saw past his tough guy facade.

"I'm worried about him too," I said softly.

The side of his mouth twitched. "Zarex can take care of himself."

"We all can," I said. "But that doesn't mean we don't need help from time to time."

Honestly, I was scared that if they couldn't use Zarex as a host, they would kill him. They might already have. I could hardly bear the thought.

"That's true," Rayax admitted. "Even I need help sometimes. That's why these jokers are here." He jerked an antenna toward Tarvun and the others.

"We could always, you know, not help," Tarvun said. He crossed his arms and propped his boots on the chair beside him. "It's pretty comfortable here. I might take a nap. Wake me when this is all over." He closed his eyes and smiled, until Navor poked him hard in the ribs with his finger.

"You're in this with us," Navor said.

Tarvun lowered his arms and opened his eyes. "Fine. You'd all get killed without me anyway."

I could easily imagine Zarex and Slek bantering in the same way. So much so it made me want to cry. I held it back and slipped out of my seat. I wandered the few steps down to the back of the pod, to E'rel's corner.

"How are things?" I asked, for lack of anything else to say.

He looked up at me and scowled. "Did you need something?"

I opened and closed my mouth a couple of times. "I just want to know whether or not whatever you're working on is going to help us."

For a moment, he looked outraged. Then his expression softened slightly. "Brinley told me humans need assurance. You don't simply believe what you're told."

"That's true," I said. "I'm sure the same can be said for any species. Do Parvorans accept every word anyone says?"

"We accept very few words anyone says," he replied. "We are taught to act, rather than wait to react."

"That sounds about right." I sat beside him and crossed my legs. "Do you need some help?"

Again, he looked outraged, then stepped himself back from it. "You could hold this while I attach that." He handed me a tube.

I held the tube while he screwed a mechanism of some kind to the end of it. He could have done it himself, but only with difficulty. It was a job for three or more hands.

"Thank you." He took back the tube and handed me another one.

"How many of these do you have?" I asked.

"Eight." He started to attach a second mechanism to the tube.

"And how long have you been trying to do this by yourself?" I eyed him over the tube.

"An hour," he said.

"Wow, I thought humans hated to ask for help." I handed him back the tube and reached for another.

"Parvorans are proud people." He sat back and exhaled through his nose.

"I've noticed that," I said without any condemnation. There was nothing wrong with being proud, even if you did waste an hour trying to do a difficult task. "Five to go."

He nodded. "Brinley also said humans often state the obvious."

I grinned. "Did you just tease me?"

"Of course not," he said. "I was just…"

"Stating the obvious?" I suggested. "It's okay to tease a little bit. It means you care." As long it wasn't nasty or intentionally hurtful. It was a fine line between teasing and bullying and some people could never tell the difference.

He looked confused at that, but got to work on the last few devices.

"What are these anyway?" I asked. "More anti-bot devices?"

"In a manner of speaking," he said. "They're to isolate the nanobots from the whole…hive. Technically they aren't a hive, because they're not alive."

I waved a hand. "I understand. It's as good a word as any. What happens then?"

"I don't know. The nanobots might leave the host. They may operate on their own. My goal is to find options, because we may need them." He looked troubled by that.

"Slek would have… would do the same thing," I said. At least, I *thought* he would. He always seemed to have a knack for producing useful devices, or messing with existing ones to make them do cool things.

"Yes." E'rel placed each of the finished mechanisms in a line with a gap between them. In the middle of each, he placed the anti-bot devices J'avet and he used on the last pod. Eight of each. "Two devices per person."

"Do you want me to hand them out?" I asked.

Before he could answer, Brinley said, "We're approaching Tarathu. There are several ships in orbit."

"Yes, do that now." E'rel took two and left me to divide the rest between the members of our team.

More than one looked doubtful that the new device would be helpful, but they added them to their holsters along with their blasters.

I just pushed one into each pocket.

"*Gamma* is increasing speed," Brinley said. "At this

rate, she'll overtake us in approximately twenty minutes."

"Let her," J'avet said. "She'll make it easier for us to hide. Set a course for the far side of Tarathu. We are a pod of Iritauri, exactly where we are supposed to be, doing what we were told. The vidscreen was damaged. If they give us orders, we follow them. "

"Unless they try to get them directly into our brains," I said.

"That can't be helped. We'll have to pretend." J'avet sat back and tried to look calm, but by now I knew him too well for that. He was as anxious as the rest of us.

"*Gamma* is two minutes out," Brinley said. "One of the Iri ships is moving to intercept."

"Us or *Gamma*?" I asked.

"I'm not sure," Brinley said. "It might be us. One minute until she catches up. Wait, brace yourselves!"

A shaft of light blossomed in the back window of the pod, heading right for us. Just when I thought it would hit, it shot over the top of us, so close I had to throw my hand over my eyes to keep from being blinded.

The laser passed over us and disappeared.

"Plot a course to evade further shots," J'avet said.

"Okay, but the Iri ship is now headed straight for

Gamma," Brinley said. "They must have decided we're friendly, because their enemy tried to hit us."

"Let's take advantage of it. Head for Tarathu. Send a message that we are damaged and need to land immediately." J'avet's mouth was set in a line. *Gamma* gave us an opportunity, but she'd brought herself under fire to do it.

I couldn't look. I didn't want to think about all those people who might die so we could succeed.

"Message sent," Brinley said. "The reply is coordinates."

"Follow them," J'avet said.

"Following," she confirmed.

A flash of light drew my attention to the rear window, followed by debris blasted in every direction.

I couldn't tell if it was *Gamma* or another ship that was completely destroyed.

"Focus," J'avet said.

I wasn't sure if he was talking to me, himself or the others. Maybe all of us.

"Approximate time to landing?"

"Twelve and a half minutes," Brinley said, her voice tight. "Twelve."

We passed through the planet's atmosphere with a shudder.

"*Gamma* singed the top of the pod," Brinley said. "Any closer and passing into the atmosphere would have caused the pod to break up. That would have sucked."

"It's a long way down," I agreed. The planet drew closer. It looked blue and green like Earth or Calig. If you'd told me it was either, I wouldn't argue.

"Just a bit," Brinley agreed.

"Prepare to veer off course for an emergency landing," J'avet said. "Everyone get strapped in and brace yourselves."

"I'm not finding a nice, flat field," Brinley said. "This is going to get bumpy." She pressed a button and an alarm started to sound.

I hurried to sit and whipped my harness into place.

"Impact in five. Four. Three. Two."

We hit the ground so hard I was jolted forward, almost hitting my head on the seat in front. I felt as though my neck would snap, but the harness held the rest of me in place.

Outside the window, the world was a blur of green and brown.

Under the pod, trees groaned and snapped, scraping along the hull like nails.

I gritted my teeth and hung on. I liked a good

roller coaster, but not like this. This felt like we'd slam into something solid at any moment and be crushed like an aluminium can.

Finally, we started to slow, before coming to a stop in the middle of a stand of trees.

"Everyone get your belongings and get off the pod." J'avet was already out of his seat, while I was still dazed.

"Edie, move!" he snapped.

I blinked. "Right." I caught his expression as I undid my harness. He still thought I should have stayed back, out of the way, but this time there was something more. Genuine concern for my safety. I wasn't just a pest. I was a pest he cared about. That was a step up.

I think.

I didn't waste time pondering the question, just grabbed my bag and followed the others out into the jungle.

"We're approximately fifty kilometres from the nearest settlement," J'avet said. "We'll need to walk there, as quickly as possible. If they think we're Iri, they may come looking. If they know we aren't, they *will* come looking. We need to be gone from here before they do."

I scanned the skies above the trees but saw nothing yet.

"J'avet, did I see a river before we stopped?" I asked.

He frowned. "I believe so. Why?"

"We could attach the tracker to a log and float it downstream," I suggested. "If they can detect it, they'll follow that and give us more time."

He grinned. Actually *grinned*. "Rayax, get the tracker from inside the pod. Carry it until we reach the river. We'll send them on a wild boar chase."

Wild boar? I remembered Slek mentioning something about taking Danec to hunt Parvoran boar. My heart skipped to think they might be on the same planet. If they were, I would find them. We had made it this far more or less uninjured, we could make it the rest of the way.

I hefted my bag onto my back and followed J'avet into the forest.

14

I WATCHED with satisfaction as the log disappeared around a bend, the tracker tied to the top with a shoelace. Technically a bootlace, but the result was the same.

I gave it a finger wave. "Bye bye. I hope you draw all the Iri to you."

J'avet watched me, but he seemed amused for once. "It should slow them down," he said. "We still need to hurry."

Without another word, he stepped back into the cover of the trees. We all followed close behind.

As fun as sending out a decoy was, I felt vulnerable out from under the cover of the canopy.

Every so often, we heard the sound of distant

engines and stopped cold. If they got any closer, only the trees would hide our location.

"We'll get as close as we can, then rest for a few hours," J'avet said. He looked frustrated. "The forest will slow us down, but it's safer."

"Haven't we done this before?" I asked, trying to keep my tone light. On Calig, we'd had Slek and Danec with us. And Humar, who complained all the way. We also hadn't known what we were up against. If I had, I might have run the other way.

"Let's not make a habit of it," J'avet growled. "All this nature. Give me a ship any day."

I smiled. "Really? I had you pegged as the outdoorsy type." Not.

"I prefer my outdoors on a plate," he replied. "Even then, the synthetic version is better."

I made a gagging sound. "Let me guess, you've never had real cheese?" Synthcheese was barely edible, but better than nothing.

Just.

"No, should I?" He looked slightly disgusted at the idea.

"Absolutely. When this is over, I'm finding us some real food. Even if I have to take you all to Earth to get it. And before you say it," I held up a hand, "I'm not staying there."

He stepped over a log and scowled as his boots sank into mud on the other side. "If it's anything like this, I see why you prefer to be on ships."

"I don't prefer ships," I said. "I prefer cities. Cities don't tend to get torpedoed into oblivion."

I looked skyward, remembering the ship that was destroyed as we entered the atmosphere. The blueish expanse couldn't tell me if it was the *Gamma*, or an Iritauri ship which was now space junk. Neither option was a great scenario. The Iri themselves were mostly innocent. Presumably some chose the life of a host, but I suspected those weren't many.

"Cities are less muddy," J'avet agreed. He pulled his boot free and found some solid ground to put it back down.

"Do you hear that?" Brinley asked. She stopped behind us. E'rel and Rayax, who walked on either side of her, froze.

I cocked my head and listened. "Sounds like another engine," I said finally.

"Heading in this direction," Navor said from the back of the pack.

"Everyone down," J'avet ordered.

I ducked to a crouch beside him and pressed myself against the trunk of a tree. Our dark clothing and packs would make us harder to see from above.

At least in theory.

The vessel drew closer. It sounded small, like a pod.

I wondered about those on board. Specifically, were any of my guys on there? It was possible, as far as I knew. They might be up there, looking, searching, ready to kill.

Okay, I could be wrong, but I'm pretty sure they would all be pissed off if they found out later they killed me. And Brinley. And the others. And, well, *anyone*.

I squeezed my eyes shut, as though somehow that would stop the pod from seeing me. To my surprise, I felt a warm hand slip into mine. I opened my eyes to see J'avet's face right in front of me.

Anyone else might have given me reassuring words, but he simply locked his eyes on mine and stayed perfectly still.

I supposed that was his way of offering reassurance. I took what I could get.

The pod almost soared right over our heads, but it stopped short at the river. It turned and moved slowly away, presumably following the course of the river's flow.

A buzz was followed by a loud explosion and what sounded like a gush of water.

"I guess they found the tracker," I whispered.

J'avet responded with a barely perceptible nod. "Yes, I think so." He seemed disappointed. Presumably he'd wanted the Iri distracted for much longer than they were. That would have been good, but it couldn't be helped.

We waited while the pod passed over the trees a few more times, back and forth in a pattern that suggested they were searching for something. Or someone. Okay, us.

Gradually, they moved away, before they set down roughly where our pod crash landed.

"When they don't find bodies, they might come looking," J'avet said. "We need to move." He let go of my hand and led the way further in the forest.

The pace was faster now, but nothing I couldn't keep up with, since the forest itself slowed us down. I would have been happy with that any other time. Today, though, I would rather push myself than get caught out here.

"We're lucky this forest is damp," Rayax remarked.

J'avet cast him a look over his shoulder.

"If it wasn't," Rayax continued, "any explosions might set it on fire."

"That's a good point," Brinley said. "I don't fancy running from a forest fire."

"Me either," I agreed.

"Quiet," J'avet hissed. "We don't know how far their sensors can reach and what sound they might detect."

Anything he might have said was drowned out by the sound of an explosion behind us.

"There goes the pod," Tarvun said.

"It was never going to fly again anyway," Brinley said with a long sigh.

"Do we have an escape plan?" I asked.

"We'll find one, now be quiet," J'avet snapped.

That didn't fill me with much confidence, but I'd have to roll with it, like I had with everything else so far.

"We should split up," Rayax said. "Half of us can lead any Iri in the wrong direction. The others can keep going."

J'avet stopped and nodded. "Rayax, Edie and Tarvun, you're with me. Brinley, you'll need to find us another ship. E'rel, you'll need to make sure it works. Navor and Hamit, keep them safe."

He all but cut off the last word and turned around to continue walking. I barely had time to give Brinley a hug before I hurried after him.

"I'm surprised you didn't send me with them," I said.

"I'm not letting you out of my sight," he said without glancing back. "You'll get yourself killed."

"I think we both know by now that isn't true," I retorted. "For example, I'm still alive." I waited, in case I'd jinxed myself, then nodded. "See?"

"For now," he replied. He stopped mid-step and turned his head slowly to one side, then the other.

I heard it too, a moment later.

A pod headed in our direction. No, I corrected myself, not quite in our direction. Close enough to make the hairs on the back of my neck stand up, but not to suggest they knew where we were, or even that we were on the planet. With any luck, they assumed they killed us when they destroyed the pod, and were heading home for an afternoon snack.

Slowly, the Iri pod circled the area. At one point, it almost passed overhead. We dropped to a crouch and waited for it to move away.

Not going for a snack then.

My heart hammered like crazy. By the time it was out of sight and hearing, I was ready to get up and run the rest of the way. I all but leapt over fallen logs and ducked under branches so fast, J'avet had to put out a hand to stop me.

"Slow down before you get yourself hurt."

"Sorry, I got a surge of adrenaline." I slowed up a bit. "I just want all of this behind us."

"We all do, but we still need to be careful." J'avet gave me that look again. The one that suggested he wasn't sure I should be here at all. Well, it was too late for that.

"The sun is starting to set," Rayax pointed out.

"Right." J'avet consulted his watch. "We're approximately two kilometres to the Iri base. This would be a good time to stop for a few hours. When it's full dark, we'll use our night visors to see our path."

He lowered his bag to the ground.

"Okay. I could use a nap." I lowered my bag beside his and sat on a patch of dry ground. I opened the neck of my bag and pulled out one of the IF's famous protein bars. When I say famous, I really mean infamous. The things tasted as good as they looked, and they looked like a piece of brick. The texture is almost as hard. Apparently they're the healthiest thing anyone in the galaxy can eat. Or almost eat. Personally, I'd kill for a burger about now.

I bit into my bar and chewed while I wondered how Brinley was doing. I saw no indication from the

Iri pod that they spotted them. That didn't mean they were safe though.

"I have a theory," Rayax said. He seemed to be enjoying his protein bar. I knew he must be flawed in some way.

"What's that?" Tarvun asked, when it became evident no one else was going to.

I had a mouthful, so I couldn't.

"I think the IF is heading here for a full blown attack on Tarathu."

I cocked my head at him sharply, but J'avet didn't look surprised.

"They think we'll fail?" I asked. That was...rude.

"I think they're hedging their bets," Rayax said. "If we succeed, they help mop up after us. If we don't, then they destroy everything."

"But the Iritauri are IF citizens when they aren't hosts," I protested.

"The Iri are a threat to the galaxy," J'avet said, his voice low.

I swung my face toward him. "You knew about this?" If he did, I might shove the rest of my protein bar up his—

"No," he said firmly. "But I suspected. The tracker was to help lead them here, but also to lead the Iri to us. If we were destroyed before the IF could rescue us, then it wouldn't be much loss to the IF."

"I resent that," Tarvun said. "I would be a great loss."

"Me too," I agreed. "At least to myself."

J'avet's mouth twitched up slightly on one side. "I didn't say I agree with them. They would get the chance to attack the Iri and say they were provoked. After that, they could justify any attack on this planet."

"They still can, if *Gamma*..." My tongue darted over my lips and I couldn't finish the sentence. I sucked in a breath. "Surely the *Infinity* would be enough of an excuse. And *Halcyon*."

"The IF is a bureaucracy," Rayax said. "It's anyone's guess why they do what they do. It means we need to work quickly, because they'll fire first and ask questions later."

"For the record, I would really object to becoming collateral damage," I said.

"We'll do all we can to ensure that doesn't happen," J'avet said.

I twisted my mouth sideways. "I suppose turning the tracker back on led the IF right here."

"It's likely, but it was a chance we had to take," J'avet said.

"*Gamma* would have told the IF," Rayax reasoned. "There's probably an armada a day or two away."

"I feel less than valued as a member of the IF," I said. "When this is over, I might have to have some words with the IF government." What sort of fuckers sent their people into what might be a trap, unconcerned about whether or not we live or die?

Oh, who was I kidding? Governments of Earth have done it since forever. The IF was no worse and no better. And, let's be real, they had the whole galaxy to think about. Eight of us were practically nothing, even if we were in my top eleven most amazing people in the galaxy.

"Get some rest," J'avet advised. "It's going to be a long night."

"Promises, promises," I said with a cheeky smile.

He smiled back and I saw in his eyes he'd rather be somewhere alone with me than out here.

Me too, buddy. Me too.

15

I ADJUSTED my visor for the tenth time in about three minutes. It didn't need adjusting, and fixing it made no difference whatsoever. It was just my nerves which made me restless, and my desire to get this over with before we were blasted to smithereens by friendly fire.

"Keep still," J'avet hissed, before he adjusted his visor. He'd done it at least as many times as I had.

I smirked, even though I knew he wouldn't see it. I would razz him about it later.

Now, I peered into the darkness and let the visor lock on the building down the slope from us. After a moment, the structure came into focus, showing me almost as much as I would see in daylight.

The best thing about the Iri was they needed

sleep as much as the rest of us. That meant the building was quiet except a handful of guards who walked this way and that.

J'avet gestured to Rayax and Tarvun and waved for them to head down to the left. He pointed to me and himself and waved to the right. He really *wasn't* going to let me out of his sight. He pulled out his anti-Iri device and nodded for us to do the same.

When he started down the slope at a slow, silent pace, I followed close behind. Not so close I would run into the back of him, but close enough.

He snuck behind a small stand of trees and we again took stock of the path ahead. Two guards stood near the corner of the building. Two stood at the opposite corner. Rayax and Tarvun would have to take care of the latter two. We would focus on the ones in front of us.

J'avet beckoned me forward and moved out again.

Barely a handful of steps from the guards, he started to trot, device in his raised hand. He pointed it right at the guard furthest from him and pressed the button on the side.

I did the same with the closer guard.

Almost in unison, they were struck down, frozen

in place. Their nanobots poured out in a flood and lay deactivated at their feet.

We caught both guards and lowered them silently to the ground. I made sure mine was more or less okay, then glanced over to see that Rayax and Tarvun had done the same with theirs.

I let out a long, slow breath. This was far from over, but we'd taken that first step. We got this.

I hoped.

J'avet nodded toward the door which led into the building. At least, I think that's what happened. His visor jerked in that direction.

I fell in behind him and managed to contain a squeal of surprise when Rayax and Tarvun appeared behind me.

Heart in my throat, I followed J'avet toward the door. I was surprised to find it open. Then again, this was a planet of Iri who more or less shared the same mind. They had no reason to keep each other out.

We stepped into an empty room. A door at the back led into another.

"I'm starting to think this building is a decoy," Rayax whispered.

I pressed my lips together. I hoped it wasn't, because it might end up being a trap.

Mice caught in it—us.

"There's something here." J'avet covered the glow of his watch with his hand, then turned it off. "Through there." He pointed his device toward the rear door.

If you get us killed, I thought in his general direction, *I'm going to be pissed.*

We stepped through the doorway, into a room larger than the one we'd left.

J'avet was right, there was something here. Or rather, someone. Several of them. They lay on the same kind of beds the ships all had in their infirmaries.

Human, Centauri, Dendran and Agusian, they were all attached to tubes like an IV, which ended at a needle in their bare arms.

"Just a guess, they're trying to figure out how to make them hosts," Rayax said. He moved between the beds.

I murmured my agreement and did the same. I couldn't hold back a short, low cry at the sight of a familiar face lying on his back, eyes closed.

"Zarex," I breathed. I put a hand to his wrist. His pulse was strong and even.

I shook him gently, mindful that he might be injured.

He didn't stir. The tube must be keeping him unconscious.

I chewed my lips. It was also possible the tube was keeping him alive. If you could call this living.

Without stopping to think further, I slid the needle out of his arm and let it fall. It slapped against the side of the bed, loud against the deafening silence.

"Zarex," I whispered in his ear. "Wake up."

For approximately a century, nothing happened. Then, finally, he stirred.

"Edie?"

I clamped a hand over his mouth to keep him from talking too loud.

"Shhh," I urged. "We need to get you out of here."

He nodded that he understood. I removed my hand.

I hadn't noticed Rayax was beside me until he clasped hands with his brother and helped him to sit.

"It's 'bout time," Zarex said, sounding sleepy.

Rayax snorted. "We need to free the rest of them too."

I nodded and left them to do their male, brotherly reunion bonding thing and started to check everyone out before pulling their needles free as well. I had to take a moment to staunch the blood each time, but there was no point in freeing them only to have them bleed to death.

J'avet and Tarvun followed me around the room, helping to keep everyone quiet as they woke.

A room full of traumatised, possibly screaming, people would draw too much attention to us.

Fortunately, everyone seemed to understand the need for silence. Or they were too scared to make a sound. Honestly, I couldn't think about it too much right then.

I finished with the last needle and helped a Centauri woman to her feet.

"Rayax, you get them out of here and into the forest. The further away they can get, the better."

"I'm staying with you," Zarex whispered.

J'avet hesitated.

I was sure under his visor he was thinking of arguing. Finally he shrugged.

"Suit yourself, but if you're weak and get us killed—"

"I won't." Zarex sounded more alert by the moment. He even managed to smile at me before I gave him a quick hug.

"It's good to see you," I whispered.

"It's good to be seen," he said. "And not be a host."

"Bonus," I agreed. "You'll have to tell me all about it later."

J'avet interrupted our moment. "Did you see enough to know where to find whoever or whatever is behind this?" he asked bluntly.

"I have a vague idea," Zarex said. "There's a bunker underneath this building. I heard them talk about it before they put me under."

"That sounds ominous," I said.

Zarex smiled and bent to kiss my forehead, above my visor. "I'd give you more, but that will have to wait until your face isn't covered."

"I look forward to it," I said.

J'avet cleared his throat. "Worry about that later." He reached into his bag for a spare visor and handed it to Zarex. "We don't have weapons to spare, so you'll have to stay close."

"I can do that." Zarex took my hand and moved so our bodies were touching.

He was incredibly distracting.

I reminded myself to focus.

By now, Rayax herded everyone else out the door. With any luck, they'd make it into the forest without being seen.

"How do we get into this underground bunker?" J'avet asked.

"Back out the door and to the left," Zarex said.

We followed J'avet with Tarvun close on our heels. Sure enough, at the end of the first room in the building was a doorway. It was so far over, our visors hadn't seen it, showing us shadows instead.

Now I *could* see it, it gave me a strange chill. It wasn't just the air, it was the impenetrable darkness beyond the doorway. Even the visors made out only vague shapes.

"Just wondering, are you sure this isn't a trap?" Tarvun asked.

"I'm almost certain it is," J'avet said. "It's also the only way to go, unless you see another?"

"Can't say I have," Tarvun said.

"Right. Be on your guard," J'avet said to us all.

From the moment I laid eyes on Zarex, I wanted to ask him... I could hardly even think about it. I wasn't sure I could handle the answer, but I had to know.

"Have you seen Slek and Danec?" I held my breath.

"Not since I arrived," Zarex said softly. "And only Slek. I haven't seen Danec since we were all on *Halcyon*."

I nodded. I *had* to believe he was alive. Slek too. Until I knew otherwise, I refused to give up hope.

"Quiet," J'avet snapped.

I froze in place.

Someone was coming, but I couldn't tell from which direction.

J'avet waved us back toward the wall, deeper into the shadows.

I gripped my anti-bot device tight in my hand, ready to use it if I needed to. Honestly, it would be all too easy to aim it in no particular direction and fire. It wouldn't do any harm to anyone friendly, and any Iri I hit would be free.

Of course, there was always the possibility I would hit nothing and end up wasting the device's power. That would leave Zarex and I both more or less defenceless, unless you count our razor sharp wits. I suspected that may not help against Iri who wanted to kill us. I would prefer to die laughing than any other way, but not today.

Heavy footsteps drew closer.

My head swam and I realised I'd held my breath for too long. I let it out and drew in another, trying to make no sound while doing it.

Nothing suggested Iri had superhuman hearing, but fear does strange things to a person's logic. Even mine. Okay, especially mine.

A shout sounded from the room we'd rescued Zarex from and a light turned on in there.

"Oops," Zarex whispered in my ear. "I think they know I left."

I smiled. Same old Zarex. It was nice to see his sense of humour was intact.

"I think they want you back," I whispered. That was too damned bad. He was mine and I wasn't going to give him up without a fight.

Zarex squeezed my hand, confirming he was in full agreement. Good. I would hate to waste time arguing over something like that, especially here.

I looked toward J'avet and wished I could see his face. I had no idea what he was thinking. Did I ever? No, but particularly now, with his face covered.

Did we run or stay put? If we ran, which way would we go?

I heard him exhale.

"We'll head underground before they find us here," he said. He sounded so decisive it gave me hope that at least someone here knew what they were doing.

He started back toward the darkened doorway and disappeared from sight.

I gripped Zarex's hand hard and stepped after

J'avet. If I was the praying kind, I might ask that we be near our goal. I had about all the excitement I could take for one night. Okay, one lifetime. When this was over, I was going to live the most boring life possible.

Yeah, right, as if the guys would let it be boring. I would settle for safe and calm, with short periods of bungee jumping, or something similar.

Once through the doorway, the visors detected a set of steps. I stopped before I fell down them and into...wherever they led.

The shouts from behind us got louder.

I glanced back. "I think we need to hurry."

"Forward," J'avet said. He took a couple of steps down and I started to follow.

Then the lights came on. They were so bright I cried out before I slammed my eyes shut and tore off my visor.

"Fucking hells," I growled. I forced my eyes back open, whirled around and blinked.

Four Iri stood looking in our direction, eyes glazed, silver skin shining in the light.

My heart leapt.

16

"DANEC," I said breathlessly. Thank whatever forces or deities might exist, he was still alive.

I was slightly less delighted about the blaster he held in his hand.

"Walk down the stairs," he ordered.

Nothing in his expression suggested he had any clue who I was, or cared. I was an intruder, along with J'avet, Zarex and Tarvun. We would be dealt with.

"Do as he says," J'avet ordered.

I turned back around. Something in the Parvoran's eyes suggested he had a reason why we shouldn't fight back. I thought of one, off the top of my head. If we deactivated the nanobots from the

Iri, four former hosts would fall down the stairs and take us with them.

Hard pass. Or hard fall. Either way, no thanks.

There was something more to it, though. As usual, J'avet gave away nothing more.

Pretending to be sulky, which wasn't difficult under the circumstances, I trudged along behind J'avet.

Every so often I glanced over my shoulder. I needed to reassure myself I wasn't seeing things. Danec was really alive. Not that I doubted it. No way. Okay, a bit. So much time had passed, it felt like another lifetime since I'd seen him last. I hoped with everything I had that he was still in there.

If he wasn't... A tear slid down my cheek, but only one. I didn't have time to break down right now. I would save that fun for later.

We reached the bottom of the stairs and stopped.

"Turn to the right," Danec ordered.

I watched J'avet for a sign we should do something.

His expression remained unchanged, he turned right.

What the fuck? He must have a plan. If he did, I hoped he'd let us in on it soon. I wasn't sure how much longer I could keep from using my anti-bot device on Danec.

We walked down a long corridor lit with a small bulb every few metres. It smelled of moisture and dank. I guess the Iri weren't too fussy about their underground bunkers.

"Well, isn't this fun?" Zarex said conversationally. "It's always nice to be around J'avet. Nothing ever goes wrong."

"It's a non-stop party," I said. I gave Zarex a look. J'avet was doing the best he could. Whatever he had in mind, would surely give us the best chance of getting out of this alive.

Right?

Zarex tilted his antennas at me as if he wasn't surprised I was defending J'avet now. I guess he saw something might happen between us, given half a chance.

"I wouldn't be anywhere else," Zarex said.

"Nor would I," J'avet said.

I frowned at the back of his head. There was a double meaning to his words. It wasn't too hard to figure it out. Let Danec show us the way. The way to where though? Hopefully not to a place they'd lock us in and throw away the key. Or simply kill us outright.

"This is definitely prime real estate," I said ironically. "It's like every baddie's underground bunker."

"How many baddie's bunkers have you been in?" Zarex asked.

"This is the first," I admitted. Hopefully the last. "You know I watch a lot of movies. Danec does too, right Danec?" I glanced back at him, but his eyes were still glazed. He gave no sign of having heard a word.

I was tempted to slap him, to see if he'd react, but I suspected he'd respond by shooting me. If he survived and was de-botted, he would have to live with that. I objected to not being around to help him through it.

"Through that doorway," Danec said. His words were redundant, because there was only one way to go.

Eyes on J'avet, I stepped through.

J'avet stopped.

My heart pounded. I waited for him to turn around and fire, but he didn't. He just... stood.

"J'avet?" I whispered.

I thought I caught the shake of his head, but I could have imagined it because I wanted to see something. *Anything.*

The room we stood in was cold and as dark as

the rest. They really didn't do 'hospitable' here. I suppose it's true what they say; it's all about location, location, location.

"It could use a coat of paint and some comfy furniture," I remarked.

Danec was unmoved. At least he wasn't pissed off. Not that I could tell, anyway.

Yet.

"It is a little empty," Zarex agreed.

"Now you mention it, it is," Tarvun agreed. "Are we waiting for something?"

"Or someone?" Zarex added.

J'avet's mouth was set in a line. Was that it? He was waiting to see what might happen?

Honestly, I wasn't a fan of playing the wait and see game, but he was the one in charge. If he knew what he was doing, then I would go along with it. What choice did I have? Okay, a few, but I would still follow his lead for now.

Footsteps approached from the direction we'd come. The sound of booted feet on the stairs, moving closer. They reached the bottom of the stairs and started down the corridor.

My hands sweated. I gave J'avet a scared look, silently begging him to know what he was doing. If he didn't, we were fucked. We'd be dead before the

IF attacked the planet. I didn't want to die in a hole in the ground. That would suck.

My heart sank when familiar faces appeared in the doorway and stepped through.

Brinley, E'rel, Hamit and Navor. They all looked tired, but in good spirits.

I frowned. Better spirits than they probably should be, considering they were prisoners of—

I gaped.

"Slek?" I send another thanks to the various deities of the universe that he too was alive. His skin was silver, but he was alive.

Shit.

I guess it was only a matter of time before the Iri made him one of them. Only—

There was something about him that didn't seem quite the same as the rest of them.

His eyes.

He looked in my direction and I saw recognition in them.

My heart leapt. I almost took a step forward, but J'avet hissed, "Don't move."

I opened my mouth to argue, but the firmness in his eyes made me close it again and stop.

To Brinley, J'avet said, "You were supposed to find a way out of here."

She smiled ruefully. "We tried, but we got a bit sidetracked by this Iri guy. He insisted we come down here." She jerked her head toward Slek.

"Move over with the rest," Danec said.

Brinley looked at him sadly, but moved to do as she was told. She stepped over to stand beside me.

"What's going on?" I said out of the corner of my mouth.

"Same shit, different day," she replied, which told me nothing. "It's good to see you're all okay."

"Yeah, you too." I was getting more and more confused. I noticed Brinley kept her hand at her side, as if she held something in it.

"Yes, we're fine," she said. "I would say I missed you, but it's good to spend some time apart."

I blinked, slightly hurt by her words. Why was she saying this? It made no sense.

"I suppose that's true," I said slowly.

"Yes," she agreed. "Sometimes you just need to *disconnect*." Her eye twitched in the direction of her hand.

It took me a moment to realise what she was trying to say. When I did, my eyes widened.

"Yes," I said slowly. "Disconnecting is good. It's not healthy to be connected all the time."

"Right. Slek found that out too." Brinley nodded toward him.

"How long should we disconnect for?" J'avet asked.

"Hmmm." Brinley looked thoughtful. "I would say about three."

J'avet nodded. "Three it is." He tapped his heel on the ground once.

Twice.

Three times.

We pulled out the devices I had helped E'rel finish and pointed them at the Iri. I aimed mine squarely at Danec and pressed the button on the side.

He jerked.

His eyes closed, then shot open again. He looked bewildered, scared.

"Please lower your blaster," I said. I had no idea how he might respond. I might provoke him into killing me. I might—

He lowered his arm.

I let out a breath through my nose, then swallowed hard and tried to get my head around all of this. "He's still Iri," I said softly.

"Yes, but he's under your control," Brinley said.

"He can go anywhere the rest can, but the hive can't tell him what to do."

I held back a sob. "How is this any better?" I asked. I wanted him and Slek to be free of the fucking bots, once and for all. "They still aren't themselves."

"We can think for ourselves," Slek said, his voice still robotic, but the words were his. "It was my idea not to get the bots out yet."

"Yeah." Navor cleared his throat. "I pulled the wrong device and disconnected him rather than de-botting. He suggested we wait."

"Okay." I drew the word out. My head swam with the implications. I stepped toward Danec and put a hand on his. "Danec? Are you in there?"

"I-I am." His stammer was the most Danec thing I ever heard and it made my throat choke up with emotion. "We need to…need to…need to."

"The nanobots make it hard to think," Slek said slowly and deliberately. "It's been longer for him."

That was true.

"Right." I exhaled.

"What do we need to do?" J'avet directed the question to all of the Iri. Or—whatever they were now. "We need to get to whoever or whatever is behind the nanobots."

Whatever? I thought. *Shit, Please don't let there be a giant computer at the centre of all of this.* That might be difficult to destroy.

Maybe it was a crazy person who hid behind a curtain, giving orders, like in *Wizard of Oz*.

"There is a place," Slek said. "Down."

"Deeper underground?" J'avet asked. "Show us."

Slek stood still.

"Show us," Navor said uncomfortably.

Slek turned away, toward the doorway.

"He only follows the orders of the person who used the device on him," Hamit said.

"I don't care," J'avet said. "As long as he leads us there. The rest of you, tell your Iri to follow, blasters in hand. We should look like prisoners."

We quickly did as he said, but I hated turning my back on Danec, even for a moment. I wanted to drink in the sight of him. His hair was longer, and his skin silver, but he was still one of the guys I loved. Slek too, but I could watch his ass as I walked. Dammit, I missed that ass.

"Did you find a way off this rock?" J'avet asked.

"Yes, we did," Brinley replied. "Slek showed us a ship we can take. It seems to be in working order."

Seems to be? Well, she would know. And Slek. I certainly wouldn't.

J'avet ran a hand over his head. I thought he might suggest Brinley and I leave, get to safety. I was ready to argue, but while his lips moved, no words came out. He must be thinking hard.

"These disconnectors can be used more than once," he said. "Navor, you have more than one connected to yours?"

"Yes," Navor replied. "At least, Slek's bots haven't regained control again."

Slek grinned. "Nope. They're pissed off about it too."

"Good," J'avet said, looking satisfied. "We may need to disconnect more."

"A lot more," I said. Wasn't that the point here? Disconnect, then free the hosts.

That reminded me of a conversation I had with Slek some time ago. "Slek, do you like being a host?"

He must have remembered the conversation, because he grimaced. "I consent to them being deactivated when the time comes. They can fuck right off."

I smiled. That was him all right, sass and all. "We'll be happy to oblige." Over my shoulder I said, "Danec, how about you?"

"I-I want them gone." His speech was strained. "When...when."

"When it's time to get rid of them?" I asked.

"Yes, when," he agreed. "We need to...to end them."

"We will," I promised. We would end every nanobot and free all the Freytauri to live their own lives again.

"We need to go that way," Slek said. He headed down the corridor to the left of the stairs, toward another set of stairs. "Time to go down."

I grinned. Same old flirty Slek, bots or no bots.

I took a deep breath and followed him down.

17

I WANT to say the deeper we went, the more inviting the place became. Maybe some pink paint here, a disco ball there. Heck, some mood music wouldn't have gone astray, either.

Instead, it was more of the same. Dark, dank and increasingly cold.

"It occurred to me," I said, halfway down a third flight of stairs. "An IF attack might not destroy this baddie bunker. We must be pretty far down."

Zarex, who managed to work his way through to walk beside me, said, "I was thinking the same thing. We would survive for a while before we ran out of air if they collapsed the entrance."

"Yeah, no thanks." I wrinkled my nose. "The Iri would die the same way."

"The nanobots might not though." He slipped his hand into mine and drew me closer to him.

"They might lie dormant for a thousand years until some well meaning Freytauri archaeologist excavates them and it starts all over again." That wasn't a cheery thought. I felt bad for the fictional, far future folk.

"We'll do what we can to make sure that doesn't happen," he assured me. "Whatever we need to do, we'll make sure they're destroyed forever."

"I know," I said. "I just…this place is getting to me, I suppose. It's so miserable here. Give me some sunshine and a nice beach any day. Or a park. Or a view of the stars. I'm not picky."

I wasn't. Weren't dungeons located underground to add to people's despair? Okay, maybe not, they were probably placed there for convenience, but additional misery was likely the result.

"You could go back out." He gave me a quick, sideways glance.

"You're starting to sound like J'avet," I told him.

"My wisdom must be rubbing off," J'avet said from ahead of us. "It's about time."

Zarex chuckled softly. "I wouldn't say that. I just want to keep Edie safe."

J'avet glanced over his shoulder. "Me too," he said softly.

"Same with me," Slek said. He sounded tired. The strain of thinking with a head full of angry bots must be draining.

"M-me t-t-to." Danec's stammer was getting worse.

"Sounds like we're all in agreement," Zarex said.

"I'm still not going back," I said. "Especially not alone."

Slek stopped a few steps from the bottom of the stairs. "The bots are more excited. We're close."

My heart skipped. I admit it, part of me wanted to turn tail and run. Get off this rock and let the IF blast it all the smithereens. What was a smithereen anyway? I would have to look it up later.

We descended more slowly now and in silence. Or as near to silence as that many people could go.

We reached the bottom of the stairs and into a better lit section of the building.

Also a more heavily populated one.

We were immediately passed by a handful of Iri, none of which spared us more than a glance. Those that did kept moving at the sight of the blasters. Clearly they thought their fellow hosts had the situation well in hand.

I would have liked to free them all on the spot, but we couldn't risk doing that here. Not yet anyway.

Regretfully, I followed Slek toward a room so bright I had to half close my eyes to let them adjust.

When they did, I gaped.

At least twenty Iri moved around the room, all with the same robotic expression. Computer banks lined the walls, flashing with lights in every colour I could think of. It was as close to a disco ball as I had seen here. Turn off the overhead lights, crank up some tunes and you had the perfect underground club. Apart from the whole baddie den vibe.

I took all of that in, in a flash. Then I was distracted by the sight of several Freytauri hunched over screens.

Freytauri.

Not Iritauri.

Their skin ranged from Danec's blue to Slek's purple and every shade in between. Truthfully, they all looked paler, like the shades were washed out slightly. Spending too much time underground will do that to a person.

"We bring you prisoners," Slek said in a robotic voice. "They helped the specimens escape from the laboratory."

Beside me, Zarex stiffened.

I guess he objected to being called a specimen. Fair enough, it was a shitty term, for sure. It made those people sound like a piece of plant.

One of the Freytauri, a woman with long, dead straight hair, turned slowly to look at us. Her eyes, cold and dead, seemed to look right through me. I had the feeling she thought more highly of pieces of plant.

"You have done well," she said, her voice so monotone she might have been a nanobot herself. "You serve the Tauri Empire well."

Uh-o, that didn't sound good.

"Tauri Empire?" I asked. I didn't think she would answer. You know, me being lower than a plant and all.

She turned to me and blinked slowly. She had lashes so long I wanted to hate her just for that. Straight hair and perfect lashes, everything I never had. I bet her nails were perfectly manicured too, but my eyes never left her face.

"The Freytauri are weak," she said slowly. That was the first sentence she said which had any inflection at all. "Biological life is weak. Enhancing life with technology makes them strong. The Tauri Empire will show the way."

"So, you're trying to make everyone into cyborgs?" I said.

"All life will be better," she stated.

"That's a matter of opinion," I said under my breath. "Can I have a word with the Emperor? He seems to have the wrong idea." I had a suspicion, which she confirmed a moment later when she drew herself up and glared at me.

"There is no Emperor," she hissed. "I am Empress Yinika."

Whatever or whoever she claimed to be, she seemed unhinged to me.

"You will serve the Empire or you will die." The other Freytauri had turned from their screens and stood beside her now.

"Do they all agree with your vision?" I nodded toward the closest of them.

"If they do not, they will become hosts," Yinika stated.

More than one Freytauri licked their lips or shuffled their feet.

"Surely they want that?" J'avet asked, addressing them. "To be enhanced. To be better."

"They will achieve that," Yinika said.

"When you learn how to control the nanobots

without them," J'avet guessed. "Or can control them separately."

"That's not so hard," Slek said with a grin. He stretched his arms out to either side.

Yinika looked at him in shock. Clearly she hadn't expected us to figure out how to separate hosts from the hive.

"How—"

The Freytauri around her looked terrified.

I might have felt sorry for them, but they were in this up to their eyeballs.

Instead, I smiled. "I guess you all get a dose of nanobots. Do you have any to spare?"

"I have a few I don't want," Slek said. He turned and looked right at me.

I took that as a cue. I raised my anti-bot device and hit the button. I expected Slek to freeze, and for the bots to flood out of him.

His eyes widened slightly, but then he grimaced and started to writhe.

"Mother of fuck," he said in clear discomfort. "That tickles."

I bit back a smile. I'd thought he was in pain, or dying, or something equally bad. Tickles sucked, but he could deal.

Yinika looked outraged at the sight of nanobots pouring out of Slek to lie on the ground at his feet.

He stepped back quickly. "There you go, they're all yours."

"Edie…" Danec's voice was a whisper.

I turned my device toward him. When he nodded, I pressed the button to finally free him from the vermin which invaded his body and held him prisoner for too long.

He twitched, but barely moved while his skin turned back to blue. His eyes watered and a couple of tears accompanied the bots on their way out.

Finally free, he sagged before Zarex caught him and helped him to stay on his feet.

"They will be reactivated," Yinika spluttered.

In one moment, Danec was leaning on Zarex. In the next, he'd leapt toward Yinika, blaster in hand, fury flashing in his eyes.

"Danec, no." I grabbed for him, he was too quick for me.

"If you kill her, you'll have to live with that," J'avet told him. "You'll be as bad as she is."

Danec stopped, blaster aimed square at Yinika's terrified face.

"Think carefully," she said coldly, having regained some of her composure. "You were better with those bots inside you. Faster, smarter, part of a hive. As a Freytauri, you were never a part of a community like the Iritauri are. The Empire nurtured you. Cared for you."

"Edie cares for me," Danec said, his voice almost as chilly as hers.

"I care for him too," Slek said. "But I don't boss him around."

"I boss him around, but I care as well," J'avet said.

I snorted a laugh.

"I haven't had much chance to boss him around, but he's a part of my community," Zarex said.

"Mine too," Brinley said. "And E'rel will when he gets to know him. Right E'rel?"

E'rel looked surprised, but he shrugged one shoulder, then nodded. "Yes, of course."

Danec smiled with one side of his mouth. "See, I don't need bots to belong."

I made a mental note to have that printed on a t-shirt, and stepped closer to Danec.

"You see how happy they are without the bots?" I said to Yinika.

"Happiness is irrelevant," she said. "Only productivity and strengthening the Empire matter."

"Said every dictator ever," I replied. "Happiness is *everything*. Without it, there's no point in living." To her co-conspirator Freytauri, I asked, "Do you want to be a mindless drone? Do you honestly think people are better off like that?"

"She … offered us power," a guy with blueish-purple skin replied slowly. "The galaxy at our feet."

"If you follow her, the galaxy is going to be at your door," I said. "Bashing it down to get in and stop you."

"An IF fleet is a couple of days away," J'avet said. "This is your last chance to surrender."

"Never," Yinika hissed. She twisted and lunged for a button on the console behind her. Before she could hit it, a flash from a blaster shot out toward her. It hit her in the centre of her chest. She let out a gurgling cry and sagged onto the console. With her fingertips, she made a last swipe at the button, but slid down the console and onto the floor.

There she lay, surrounded by nanobots.

Danec looked stunned.

For a moment, I thought he shot her. Then I saw a blaster in J'avet's hand and satisfaction on his face.

"Now *you* have to live with it," I said softly.

His brows rose slightly. "Better me than Danec."

I wasn't sure it was that simple, but it was done now.

"I'll accept unconditional surrender from all of you," J'avet said to the remaining baddies.

I couldn't think of them any other way. They were all complicit.

"You have mine," the man said.

"And mine," a weary-looking woman agreed.

"Mine also," said a third.

Before anyone else could speak or move, a ripple passed through Yinika's body. The hole in her chest, where she was hit by the blaster, became wider and wider. A trickle of nanobots drained out of her, onto the floor. The trickle became a flood. They headed for the consoles and started to eat through the metal.

"I think we need to switch these off," I said.

"Now," J'avet said. He swapped his blaster for his anti-bot device and started to fire. "Is there a master switch?"

"Yes," the Freytauri man said. "Over on the—"

"Just use the fucking thing," J'avet snapped.

"Yes, of course." The man stepped carefully around the bots and hurried to the console on the other side of the room.

J'avet and Zarex followed and I was close behind. Danec slid a hand into one of mine and Slek moved in close enough for our arms to touch.

"We have company," Brinley said.

I glanced toward the door. Every Iri in the complex looked to have congregated and were pushing through the door toward us. The ones who had already been in the room formed a half circle around us.

"Quickly," J'avet snapped.

The man nodded. "This will take two to three minutes."

"We might not have that long." J'avet waved Slek and E'rel over. "Help him. The rest of you, use your devices."

I turned so my back was to Slek and fired off a few shots from the anti-bot device. I missed one, but hit three who froze, slowing down the Iri behind them until they fell. The Iri stepped over them, only to be shot as well.

The bunker creaked.

The nanobots ate their way up the console, almost to the ceiling. Their numbers were double, maybe triple by now.

"Faster," J'avet snapped. "They'll bring this place down around us."

"Almost there," Slek said. "It's a complicated algorithm, but I see what he's doing."

"No, not that," E'rel said.

I was curious what he was referring to, but too

busy shooting at Iri to stop and look.

"Take that," I said as I got one in the chest. "And that. I wish we had more devices." I aimed at an Iri woman, but my device clicked and nothing happened. "I'm out of juice."

"So am I," Navor said. He switched to his disconnector, so I did the same.

It slowed down the first few Iri, but their numbers seemed to grow, rather than die down. They must be pouring down the stairs. That would have to stop soon, right?

"Are we there yet?" I asked in my best exhausted, fed up voice.

"In five," Slek said.

"Four."

"Three."

"Two."

"One."

I waited.

The Iri kept on coming.

"Slek?"

"Sorry, now it's one," he replied.

A second later, every Iri in the room stopped dead. The nanobots went still.

I held my breath.

Let it out.

An eerie silence fell over the room until it was broken by the groans of Freytauri as the bots fell dead on the floor. Hundreds, thousands.

In moments the floor resembled a shining beach, covered in black sand. It crunched with every step anyone took.

I sagged and lowered my devices.

"As far as I can work out, that will have deactivated every bot in the galaxy," Slek stated.

"Thank you to whoever put in a kill switch," I said. They must have realised the bots might get out of hand. I wasn't sure Yinika realised the extent of the trouble they would cause.

But then again, I wasn't sure she was in control. The bots inside her must have found a way to use her to do their work. She might have been as innocent as the Iri.

It didn't matter now, I supposed, she was as dead as the bots.

"Everyone take a few minutes to rest," J'avet said. "We'll need it to get everyone out of here."

Everyone was also going to need a shit load of therapy after this. Especially Danec, who pulled me into his arms and held me like he had no intention of ever letting go.

I wasn't sure I would let him go either, so I was

okay with that.

"Are you all right?" I asked in his ear.

"I am now," he said. "I'm so sorry about…everything. Doctor Mazic…"

"That was the bots, not you," I said firmly. "You wouldn't hurt a fly."

"A what?" he asked.

I snorted. "It doesn't matter. The point is, you wouldn't hurt anyone."

"I would have shot Yinika." He sounded so hurt my heart broke a little.

"I'm not sure she was a person anymore," I said. "She was more bot than anything. I don't think J'avet will feel too bad about it."

"I suppose." He rested his cheek on the side of my head.

"I missed you," I said softly. "Obviously. I did come all the way out here to save your ass." Speaking of that, I cupped his butt and gave it a squeeze.

"Thank you. I'll spend forever showing you how grateful I am for that."

"Me too." Slek wrapped his arms around us both. "I was not host material. I told them that. Do you think they listened?"

"I'm guessing not," I said and gave him a slight

smile. "They didn't seem big on independence and consent."

"Yeah, they really weren't," Slek agreed. "Hey, J'avet, can we get out of here now?"

"Do you all need a reminder of how to speak to me with respect?" J'avet rubbed the side of his face. He looked like a guy who had the weight of the galaxy on his shoulders.

I suppose he had.

"Naw," Slek replied. "I never knew, and I'm okay with that."

J'avet grimaced and shook his head.

"I don't think I'm cut out for military life," Danec said. "I may retrain as a librarian, or something less exciting."

"Hey, books are exciting," I protested. And a metric fuckton safer than this.

"They are," Slek agreed. "So, about getting out of here."

J'avet nodded sharply. "Those who can, help those who need it. We'll go slowly if we have to, but everyone leaves here in one shot. No one is coming back down here. Ever."

I let Danec go and reached a hand out to a young Freytauri woman who looked dazed and pale.

"Come on," I said in my best cheery nurse voice. "Let's get you out of here."

She nodded her thanks and let me put an arm around her shoulders.

A mass of slow-moving bodies, we made our way to the stairs as a loud bang rocked the bunker.

The ground began to shake.

"Shit," J'avet muttered. "So much for the IF being two days away."

18

"Wait, what?" I stared at him for half a second before he waved us to keep going.

"Everyone get out!" he shouted. "As fast as you can. We have no time to waste. But don't stampede!" he added as the mass of Freytauri began to panic and rush at the stairs.

They pushed and shoved and several were almost knocked to the ground.

"Anyone else who shoves, I will use my blaster on you," J'avet growled.

They slowed slightly after that, enough to move up the stairs like a swarm of ants escaping their flooded nest.

Another explosion sounded from above and the

whole place shook. Rock, dirt and other debris rained down on us.

"I didn't come this far to get buried alive," I said under my breath. I willed everyone to hurry, but to do it carefully. Since those things didn't go so well together, I hoped we'd make it out in one piece.

We reached the top of the first set of stairs as a third blast shook the bunker. A chunk of rock narrowly missed my head, but struck my shoulder before it bounced into the wall and crashed to the floor.

Tears of pain filled my eyes. I felt warm wetness on my upper arm, but didn't have time right now for a good look. I wasn't injured so badly I needed to stop. That was all that mattered.

"Edie?" I hadn't realised Zarex was right behind me until he spoke.

"I'm fine," I said firmly. To the Freytauri woman I supported with my good arm, I said, "We're almost there." She probably knew the place better than I did, but my words seemed to offer her some reassurance.

We reached the second flight of stairs and started up. Why do baddies need to build underground bunkers? A nice little cottage beside the beach would make a nice lair, surely? Or a chalet beside a lake. If I was a baddie, I would definitely have a chalet. Or a chateau. No underground *anything*.

The lights went out.

"Fuck." I turned on the light on my phone with the end of my nose—a trick that usually didn't work. Go me.

It didn't illuminate much, but as others turned their own watches on, it gave us enough light to stagger up the last flight.

I might have imagined a hint of daylight, but I clung to that with every bit of hope I had left.

My legs burned with the effort of walking up so many steps. I wouldn't need to go to the gym tomorrow anyway. I hadn't had such a good workout since—ever. Honestly, I'd be happy if I never had another one like it.

The press of bodies surged forward and I was almost pushed to my knees. At the last moment, I caught myself and trudged up the last few steps and into the open of the top floor of the building.

"Everyone out," J'avet ordered. He tapped his watch. "IF ships in orbit, this is Commander J'avet. Cease your attack on Tarathu *immediately*."

Okay, I admit it, his bossy tone was kinda hot. Also the fact he was trying to stop us from getting killed.

The sky lit up with another laser, which struck the building with a deafening crack.

"We might be too close to the building for comms to work," Slek said.

"Or they ignored us," Zarex added. He turned on his own watch and repeated the message, but with his own name.

Finally, a voice responded.

"How do we know it's you and not a bot?"

Legit question, I thought. Unfortunately.

"Because it's me!" J'avet all but shouted into his watch.

Another laser shot out of the sky. It hit the building square on. Everything went silent, then the ground started to shake.

The building crumbled. It imploded in on itself and disintegrated into the levels below it. Soon all that remained was a hole in the ground.

"Well fuck, that could have been us," I said.

"We need to get out in the open," J'avet said. "Somewhere they can see us."

"If they bother to look." I hadn't seen Zarex look worried before, but he did now. And scared. Fair enough; I was about ready to pee my pants.

"What about the ship Brinley found?" I asked. "Can we get off here?"

"Not without the IF shooting us down," J'avet said. He didn't look scared, he looked furious. "We need to convince the IF we're us, or they'll keep on shooting."

As if on cue, another laser blasted a small building close by.

"There's a field that way." Slek pointed east. "Away from any ships or buildings. Away from anywhere they might aim, hopefully."

"Lead the way," J'avet said.

Normally Slek would stop for a wisecrack, but not today. Now, he simply led us at a slow jog away from the buildings, toward what looked to be farmland. If it wasn't for lasers from the sky, it would be a nice place to rest for a day or three. Maybe build a cottage. Import some cows and chickens.

Another laser took out another building.

"The nanobots have all been deactivated," J'avet was saying into his watch. "If you look at your scanners, you'll see several hundred Freytauri, a couple of Parvorans, some Agusians, a Garvian or two and some humans. IF citizens, every one of us. No Iritauri."

"Stand by," a voice replied.

"Standing by," J'avet muttered angrily.

We reached the middle of a field of grain and

many of us flopped to the ground, too tired to move another step, or even stand. If the IF didn't believe us, we were dead anyway, so we might as well be comfortable.

I leaned again Danec, who looked utterly spent. The Freytauri I was helping leaned against me.

We waited.

"Commander J'avet." A new voice came through both his watch and Zarex's.

I jerked upright. "Captain Marshall?" Relief flooded through me. I didn't know how the *Gamma* survived and I didn't care. I was just happy it had.

"This is J'avet," he said simply. "Good to hear a voice we recognise." He didn't add, 'and who recognises me.' The sentiment was obvious.

"Commander Zarex here too, Captain." Zarex sounded cheerful but he, too, looked tired.

I suspected I only knew a fraction of what he'd been through in the last few weeks. Only now, out in the light, I saw bruises which had almost faded on his cheeks and neck. His antennas were intact, but they both drooped slightly as though showing his exhaustion in a way the rest of him couldn't.

"Nice to hear your voice too," Marshall said. "J'avet says you're all bot-free."

Slek leaned over and spoke into Zarex's watch. "Bot-free and feelin' fine."

"Reports are coming in of deactivated nanobots all over the galaxy," Marshall said. "Was that anything to do with you?"

Slek, in true Slek style, pretended she was giving him the chance to claim all the glory. "That was everything to do with me, Captain, but I had a bit of help from my friends."

J'avet rolled his eyes, but almost smiled. "We would appreciate it if you didn't destroy all the ships, so we can get off this planet."

"We thought about that," Marshall said slowly.

My heart sank. Surely the IF wasn't going to leave us out here, alone, with no way off? I mean, I guess we could make a life here, if we had to. I had my guys and Brinley, crops, water...

"We thought we'd bring *Gamma* to you," Marshall finished.

The ship burst through the atmosphere above us and began a slow descent.

"Yeah, that works," I said to myself. "As long as they actually believe it's us." I waved skyward for good measure.

A few others did as well. Since the *Gamma* didn't

fire on us, presumably they knew we were friendly. Well, most of us anyway. E'rel had a way to go. He currently sat beside Brinley, close enough to touch.

They talked in low voices I couldn't overhear, but I wasn't trying hard.

I leaned against Danec again and he put an arm around me.

"I thought about you," he said softly. "Every time I was able to think for myself. Sometimes the bots were listening for orders, or waiting. Then, it was like they looked away for a moment. I wanted to run away from them, but I couldn't move unless they wanted me to. I was…" He sniffed.

"I know," I said softly. I didn't really know, but I could imagine how it might feel to be stuck in your own body. It sounded pretty shit, to be honest.

"If there's ever anything I can do to help you," I said. "Anything to get you through the pain."

"Just be here," he said. He leaned in to press a soft kiss against my mouth. "That's all I need."

"I can be here," I said, "as long as it's not *here*. Anywhere but this planet."

He gave a short, bitter laugh. "Yes, anywhere but here would be great."

"Very great," I agreed. I glanced up. "It won't be

long now." I wasn't sure I wanted to be on another ship, but if it meant escaping Tarathu, I would take it.

I took a breath and got to my feet. Danec stood beside me, with Slek on the other side. After a moment, J'avet joined us and Zarex a hair behind him.

At that moment, I realised something. It was almost over. Everything we'd gone through since Danec and I met, all the craziness and heartbreak. The separations and worry. I wanted to cry, or get really, really drunk. Maybe both.

We stepped back to give *Gamma* more room, even though she had plenty. She kicked up a bunch of dirt and wind as she lowered her struts and landed in the field. From here, she looked huge.

I suppose she was, compared to me. I didn't mind feeling small, she would have to evacuate a lot of people from the planet. We'd be lying on top of each other, so to speak, but I don't think anyone would mind too much. At least for the first while.

Gamma settled on the ground and a ramp lowered slowly. When it was in place, the door slid aside.

As expected, several security officers stepped out

first, blasters in hand. Those were lowered when Tarvun walked forward, followed by Rayax. The 'specimens,' as Yinika had called them, must have seen the ship and hurried out from wherever they'd hidden. The forest nearby, perhaps.

"Come on," J'avet said. Where once he'd have strode on ahead, he now waited for the four of us to move forward with him. Or he wanted us there to hide behind, but I didn't think that was it.

Marshall nodded to us when we drew close enough. "I see you succeeded at your mission," she said.

"Yes, we did," J'avet said. "I see the IF had enough faith in us to hold off on the attack for a while." His expression was as bitter as his tone.

Marshall shrugged. "The order came from above me. I told them to stop when I heard your voice. I wasn't sure they would listen. Lucky for you, they did."

"Lucky for all of us," I said dryly. "The IF would have killed a lot of its own people."

"Yes," Marshall replied. "They gave me an hour to evacuate the planet before they resume firing. They don't want to leave any chance of the nanobots becoming a problem in the future."

I didn't think they would be, but I said nothing. It wasn't like I would be listened to anyway.

The IF would do what the IF did, and I would have to do what I did.

In this case, that was to ask, "Please tell me you have coffee on board."

19

"UH, FUCK YEAH." I cradled the mug in my hands and inhaled the smell. Marshall was kind enough to give me a spoonful of coffee from her own stash. Even with synthmilk and whatever passed for sugar out here, it smelled like pure heaven. The fact all my guys were here in one place made this perfect. As perfect as sharing a tiny bunk room with Brinley, E'rel and two former hosts could be.

Slek smiled. "I feel the same way about this." He held up his half eaten sandwich.

Sometimes it's all about the small things.

I closed my eyes and sipped my coffee. It wasn't the best cup I ever had, but it tasted amazing.

Zarex sat against the wall, eyes half closed. "So the IF has ordered Yinika's companions to be locked in the brig until they can be interrogated properly. They've all been talking. A lot. I don't think that will save them from a lifetime in prison."

I couldn't bring myself to feel bad, frankly. They could rot there for all I cared. I only wanted to know one thing.

"What about this Tauri Empire she went on about?" I asked. "Is that a thing?"

"They all agree it was just her dream. Or the nanobots inside her," J'avet said. "They seem to have been some of the original ones who were banned so long ago. Somehow they hijacked her and made her do everything."

"At least she had that as an excuse," I said. "The others didn't. Unless they had bots too?"

"If they did, they deactivated along with the rest, but I think it was all their own actions. The kill switch was something the one who helped us put in. According to him, Yinika didn't know."

I frowned. "Why didn't he use it?"

J'avet scratched behind his ear. "I suspect he was scared it wouldn't work. Or at least, not fast enough that he wasn't killed while he waited."

Zarex made a sound of agreement. "They were all terrified of Yinika. She seemed to know everything that went on."

"Not everything," Slek pointed out.

"Enough of everything," Danec said. "The nanobots were scared of her too. Or, not her..." He looked uncertain.

"The idea of her," Slek said. "What she and her bots represented."

"Yes, that," Danec agreed. He and Slek exchanged a look.

I liked that they got along, but I hated that they had something so horrible in common. At least they had each other for support. They would both need it.

Silence fell for a long moment.

"Are we all going to Agus?" Zarex asked, breaking it.

"I am if you guys are," I said.

"I am," Danec said softly. "I have decided I will retrain. I think I'll go into something easy, like engineering."

"Hey," Slek protested. "Engineering is not easy, I —" He stopped when he realised Danec was teasing. He patted his shoulder. "I can teach you everything I know."

Danec smiled briefly. The first one I'd seen from him since he was freed. "I'd like that."

"I'm going too," Zarex agreed. "I'll be teaching computer stuff."

I grinned. "That's wonderful."

All eyes turned to J'avet. His brows rose. "You would all get into trouble if I wasn't there."

I laughed. "More like we'll follow you into it."

He snorted, but didn't deny it.

"This works out perfectly, because I've decided which of you I want to choose," I said.

Now all eyes were on me.

I let them wait for a while, then cleared my throat.

"I've decided I can't choose between you, so I want to choose you all. If that's okay with you guys?"

I held my breath while they looked at each other.

"Works for me," Slek said finally.

"And me," Danec said.

"You know how I feel," Zarex said. "If they all give you what you need that I can't, then I'm in."

J'avet sighed. "I told you you're mine. I'm not letting you go. Besides, I'm getting used to you all."

"I think that's his way of saying he likes you," I said. "That's great, because I love all of you."

"We love you too," Slek said.

All the other guys nodded and gave me fond smiles.

"How long is this journey?" I asked. "Because it's

going to be a long time before I'm alone with any of you."

"We'll find a way," Slek said. "We always do."

"Yeah," I agreed. Whatever we had to endure, we always found a way to get through it. Together, we could survive pretty much anything.

I sipped my coffee and smiled. We could take on the galaxy.

THE END.

JUST FOR YOU, I'd like to give you an exclusive, reverse harem novella. Get yours now.

IF YOU LIKED THIS BOOK, leave a review. If you loved this book, and want to read more about Edie and her alien mates, tell your friends. If enough people love it, then the galaxy is the limit.

Thanks for reading!

ABOUT THE AUTHOR

Maggie Alabaster writes reverse harem and, para-normal, sci-fi and fantasy romance.

She lives in NSW, Australia with one spouse, two daughters, one dog, and countless birds.

Sign up for my newsletter! Sign Up!

Join my reader group! Join here!

Follow me on Bookbub! Click here to follow me!

Check out my website- www.maggiealabaster.com

Book 1 Summoned by Fire

Book 2 Summoned by Fate

Book 3 Summoned by Desire

Shifter's Vault

Book 1 Discarded

Book 2 Deceived

Book 3 Disgraced

My Alien Mates

Book 1 Star Warriors

Book 2 Star Defenders

Book 3 Star Protectors

Academy of Modern Magic

Book 1 Digital Magic

Book 2 Virtual Magic

Book 3 Logical Magic

Complete Collection

Summer's Harem

Book 1: Shimmer

Book 2: Glimmer

Book 3: Flicker

Complete collection

Short reads

Taken by the Snowmen

Jingle All the Way

Also by Maggie Alabaster and Erin Yoshikawa

Caught by the Tide

Book 1–Pursued by Shadows

Book 2 Pursued by Darkness

Book 3 Pursued by Monsters